Richard Le Gallienne, Izaak Walton

The Complete Angler

The contemplative man's Recreation

Richard Le Gallienne, Izaak Walton

The Complete Angler
The contemplative man's Recreation

ISBN/EAN: 9783337400316

Printed in Europe, USA, Canada, Australia, Japan

Cover: Foto ©Andreas Hilbeck / pixelio.de

More available books at **www.hansebooks.com**

THE
COMPLETE ANGLER;

OR,

THE CONTEMPLATIVE MAN'S RECREATION.

By ISAAK WALTON.

BEING A

𝔉acsimile 𝔔eprint of t𝔥e 𝔉irst 𝔈dition pu𝔟li𝔰𝔥e𝔡 in 1653. 𝔚it𝔥 a 𝔓reface 𝔟y

RICHARD LE GALLIENNE.

LONDON:
ELLIOT STOCK.

NEW YORK:
DODD, MEAD & COMPANY.
1897.

PREFACE.

*T*HE "*first edition*" *has been a favourite theme for the scorn of those who love it not.* " *The first edition—and the worst!*" *gibes a modern poet, and many are the true lovers of literature entirely insensitive to the accessory, historical or sentimental, associations of books. The present writer possesses a copy of one of Walton's Lives, that of Bishop Sanderson, with the author's donatory inscription to a friend upon the title-page. To keep this in his little library he has undergone willingly many privations, cheerfully faced hunger and cold rather than let it pass from his hand; yet, how often when, tremulously, he has unveiled this treasure to his visitors, how often has it been examined with undilating eyes, ana cold, unenvious hearts! Yet so he must confess himself to have looked upon a friend's superb first edition of "Pickwick," though surely not without that measure of interest which all, save the quite unlettered or unintelligent, must feel in seeing the first visible shape of a book of such resounding significance in English literature.*

Such interest may, without fear of denial, be claimed for a facsimile of the first edition of "The Compleat Angler," after "Robinson Crusoe" perhaps the most popular of English classics. Thomas Westwood, whose gentle poetry, it is to be feared, has won but few listeners, has drawn this fancy picture of the commotion in St. Dunstan's Churchyard on a May morning of the year 1653, when Richard Marriott first published the famous discourse, little dreaming that he had been chosen for the godfather of so distinguished an immortality. The lines form an epilogue to twelve beautiful sonnets à propos of the bi-centenary of Walton's death :

> " *What, not a word for thee, O little tome,*
> *Brown-jerkined, friendly-faced—of all my books*
> *The one that wears the quaintest, kindliest looks—*
> *Seems most completely, cosily at home*
> *Amongst its fellows.   Ah ! if thou couldst tell*
> *Thy story—how, in sixteen fifty-three,*
> *Good Master Marriott, standing at its door,*
> *Saw Anglers hurrying—fifty—nay, three score,*
> *To buy thee ere noon pealed from Dunstan's bell :—*
> *And how he stared and . . . shook his sides with glee.*
> *One story, this, which fact or fiction weaves.*
> *Meanwhile, adorn my shelf, beloved of all—*
> *Old book ! with lavender between thy leaves,*
> *And twenty ballads round thee on the wall.*"

Whether there was quite such a rush as this on its publishing day we have no certain knowledge, though Westwood, in his " Chronicle of the Compleat Angler," speaks of " the almost immediate sale of the entire edition." According to Sir Harris Nicolas, it was thus advertised in The Perfect Diurnall: from Monday, May 9th, to Monday, May 16th, 1653 :

" The Compleat Angler, or the Contemplative Man's Recreation, being a discourse of Fish and Fishing, not unworthy the perusal of most Anglers, of 18 *pence price.   Written by Iz. Wa.   Also the*

known *Play of the Spanish Gipsee, never till now published: Both printed for Richard Marriot, to be sold at his shop iu Saint Dunstan's Churchyard, Fleet street."*

And it was thus calmly, unexcitedly noticed in the Mercurius Politicus : from Thursday, May 12, to Thursday, May 19, 1653 : *" There is newly extant, a Book of* 18d. *price, called the Compleat Angler, or the Contemplative Man's Recreation, being a discourse of Fish and Fishing, not unworthy the perusal of most Anglers. Printed for Richard Marriot, to be sold at his shop in St. Dunstan's Churchyard, Fleet street."*

Thus for it, as for most great births, the bare announcement sufficed. One of the most beautiful of the world's books had been born into the world, and was still to be bought in its birthday form—for eighteen-pence.

In 1816, Mr. Marston calculates, the market value was about £4 4s. In 1847 Dr. Bethune estimated it at £12 12s. In 1883 Westwood reckoned it "from £70 to £80 or even more," and since then copies have fetched £235 and £310, though in 1894 we have a sudden drop at Sotheby's to £150 —which, however, was more likely due to the state of the copy than to any diminution in the zeal of Waltonian collectors, a zeal, indeed, which burns more ardently from year to year.

Sufficiently out of reach of the poor collector as it is at present, it is probable that it will mount still higher, and consent only to belong to richer and richer men. And thus, in course of time, this facsimile will, in clerical language, find an increasing sphere of *usefulness; for it is to those who have more instant demands to satisfy with their hundred-pound notes that this facsimile is designed to bring consolation. If it is not the rose itself, it is a photographic reflection of it, and it will undoubtedly give its possessor a sufficiently faithful idea of its original.*

But, apart from the satisfaction of such curiosity, the facsimile has a literary value, in that it differs very materially from succeeding editions. The text by which "The Compleat Angler" is generally known is that of the fifth edition, published in 1676, the last which Walton corrected and finally revised, seven years before his death. But in the second edition (1655) the book was already very near to its final shape, for Walton had enlarged it by about a third, and the dialogue was now sustained by three persons, Piscator, Venator and Auceps, instead of two—the original "Viator" also having changed his name to "Venator." Those interested in tracing the changes will find them all laboriously noted in Sir Harris Nicolas's great edition. Of the further additions made in the fifth edition, Sir Harris Nicolas makes this just criticism: "It is questionable," he says, "whether the additions which he then made to it have increased its interest. The garrulity and sentiments of an octogenarian are very apparent in some of the alterations; and the subdued colouring of religious feeling which prevails throughout the former editions, and forms one of the charms of the piece, is, in this impression, so much heightened as to become almost obtrusive."

There is a third raison d'être for this facsimile, which to name with approbation will no doubt seem

*impiety to many, but which, as a personal predilection,
I venture to risk—there is no Cotton! The relation
between Walton and Cotton is a charming incongruity
to contemplate, and one stands by their little fishing-
house in Dovedale as before an altar of friendship.
Happy and pleasant in their lives, it is good to see
them still undivided in their deaths—but, to my mind,
their association between the boards of the same book
mars a charming classic. No doubt Cotton has
admirably caught the spirit of his master, but the
very cleverness with which he has done it increases
the sense of parody with which his portion of the book
always offends me. Nor can I be the only reader of
the book for whom it ends with that gentle benediction
—"And upon all that are lovers of virtue, and dare
trust in his providence, and be quiet, and go a
Angling"—and that sweet exhortation from* 1 *Thess.*
iv. 11—" *Study to be quiet.*"

*After the exquisite quietism of this farewell, it is
distracting to come precipitately upon the fine gentleman with the great wig and the Frenchified airs.
This is nothing against* "*hearty, cheerful Mr. Cotton's
strain,*" *of which, in Walton's own setting and in his
own poetical issues, I am a sufficient admirer. Cotton
was a clever literary man, and a fine engaging figure
of a gentleman, but, save by the accident of friendship,
he has little more claim to be printed along with
Walton than the gallant Col. Robert Venables, who,
in the fifth edition, contributed still a third part,
entitled* " *The Experienc'd Angler: or, Angling
Improv'd. Being a General Discourse of Angling,*"
*etc., to a book that was immortally complete in its
first.*

While "The Compleat Angler" was regarded mainly as a text-book for practical anglers, one can understand its publisher wishing to make it as complete as possible by the addition of such technical appendices; but now, when it has so long been elevated above such literary drudgery, there is no further need for their perpetuation. For I imagine that the men to-day who really catch fish, as distinguished from the men who write sentimentally about angling, would as soon think of consulting Izaak Walton as they would Dame Juliana Berners. But anyone can catch fish—can he, do you say?—the thing is to have so written about catching them that your book is a pastoral, the freshness of which a hundred editions have left unexhausted,—a book in which the grass is for ever green, and the shining brooks do indeed go on for ever.

RICHARD LE GALLIENNE.

Being a Discourse of

FISH and FISHING,

Not unworthy the perusal of most *Anglers*.

Simon Peter *said, I go a fishing : and they said, We also wil go with thee.* John 21.3.

London, Printed by *T. Maxey* for Rich. Marriot, in S. Dunstans Churchyard Fleetstreet, 1653.

To the Right Worſhipful

JOHN OFFLEY

Of MADELY Manor in the
County of *Stafford*, Eſq;
My moſt honoured Friend.

SIR,

I Have made
ſo ill uſe of
your former
favors, as by
them to be
encouraged to intreat that
they may be enlarged to the
patronage and protection
of this *Book*; and *I* have
put on a modeſt confidence,

A 2　　　that

The Epistle

that I shall not be denyed,
because 'tis a discourse of
Fish and Fishing, which
you both know so well, and
love and practice so much.

You are assur'd (though
there be ignorant men of an
other belief) that Angling
is an Art, and you know that
Art better then any that I
know: and that this is truth,
is demoſtrated by the fruits
of that pleasant labor which
you enjoy when you purpose
to give reſt to your mind,
and deveſt your self of your

more

more serious busineß, and
(which is often) dedicate a
day or two to this Recreation.

At which time, if com-
mon Anglers should attend
you, and be eye-witnesses of
the succeßs, not of your fortune, but your skill, it would
doubtleß beget in them an
emulation to be like you, and
that emulation might beget
an industrious diligence to be
so: but I know it is not atain-
able by common capaci-
ties.

A 3   Sir,

The Epistle

Sir, this pleasant curio-
sitie of Fish and Fishing (of
wch you are so great a Master) has been thought wor-
thy the pens and practices
of divers in other Nations,
which have been reputed
men of great Learning and
Wisdome; and amongst
those of this Nation, I remember Sir Henry Wot-
ton (a dear lover of this
Art) has told me, that his
intentions were to write a
discourse of the Art, and in
the praise of Angling, and
doubtless

doubtleß he had done so, if
death had not prevented
him; the remembrance of
which hath often made me
sorry; for, if he had lived to
do it, then the unlearned
Angler (of which I am one)
had seen some Treatise of
this Art worthy his perusal,
which (though some have
undertaken it) I could never yet see in English.

But mine may be thought
as weak and as unworthy
of common view: and I do
here freely confeß, that I

The Epistle, &c.

should rather excuse my self, then censure others my own Discourse being liable to so many exceptions; against which, you (Sir) might make this one, That it can contribute nothing to your knowledge; and lest a longer Epistle may diminish your pleasure, I shal not adventure to make this Epistle longer then to add this following truth, That I am really,   Sir,

Your most affectionate Friend,
and most humble Servant,

Iz. Wa.

TO THE
Reader of this Discourse:

Bᴜᴛ especially,
To the honeſt Aɴɢʟᴇʀ.

I Think fit to tell thee theſe following truths; that I did not under-take to write, or to pub-liſh this diſcourſe of *fiſh* and *fiſhing*, to pleaſe my ſelf, and that I wiſh it may not diſpleaſe others; for, I have confeſt there are many defects in it. And yet, I cannot doubt, but that by it, ſome readers may receive ſo much *profit* or *pleaſure*, as if they be not very buſie men, may make it not unworthy the time of their peruſall; and this is all the confidence that I can

put

put on concerning the merit of this Book.

And I wish the Reader also to take notice, that in writing of it, I have made a recreation, of a recreation; and that it might prove so to thee in the reading , and not to read *dull,* and *tedioufly* , I have in severall places mixt some innocent Mirth; of which, if thou be a severe, sowr complexioned man , then I here disallow thee to be a competent Judg. For Divines say, *there are offences given*; and *offences taken, but not given.* And I am the willinger to justifie this *innocent Mirth,* becaufe the whole difcourfe is a kind of picture of my owne difpofition, at leaft of my difpofition in fuch daies and times as I allow my felf, when honeft *Nat.* and *R. R.* and I go a fifhing together; and let me adde this , that he that likes not the difcourfe, fhould like the pictures of the *Trout* and

and other fifh, which I may commend, becaufe they concern not
my felf.

And I am alfo to tel the Reader,
that in that which is the more ufefull part of this difcourfe; that is to
fay, the obfervations of the *nature*
and *breeding*, and *feafons*, and *catching of fifh*, I am not fo fimple as not
to think but that he may find exceptions in fome of thefe; and
therefore I muft intreat him to
know, or rather note, that feverall
Countreys, and feveral Rivers alter the *time* and *manner* of fifhes
Breeding; and therefore if he bring
not candor to the reading of this
Difcourfe, he fhall both injure me,
and poffibly himfelf too by too many Criticifms.

Now for the Art of catching fifh;
that is to fay, how to make a man
that was none, an Angler by a
book: he that undertakes it, fhall
undertake a harder task then *Hales*,
that

that in his printed Book * under-took by it to teach the Art of Fencing, and was laught at for his labour. Not but that fomething ufefull might be obferved out of that Book; but that Art was not to be taught by words; nor is the Art of Angling. And yet, I think, that moft that love that Game, may here learn fomething that may be worth their money, if they be not needy: and if they be, then my advice is, that they forbear; for, I write not to get money, but for pleafure; and this difcourfe boafts of no more: for I hate to promife much, and fail.

But pleafure I have found both in the *fearch* and *conference* about what is here offered to thy view and cenfure; I wifh thee as much in the perufal of it, and fo might here take my leave; but I will ftay thee a little longer by telling thee, that whereas it is faid by many, that in *Fly-fifhing*

for

* Called the private School of defence.

for a *Trout*, the Angler muſt obſerve his twelve Flyes for every Month; I ſay, if he obſerve that, he ſhall be as certain to catch fiſh, as they that make Hay by the fair dayes in Almanacks, and be no ſurer: for doubtleſs, three or four *Flyes* rightly made, do ſerve for a *Trout* all *Summer*; and for *Winter-flies*, all *Angters* know, they are as uſeful as an *Almanack* out of date.

Of theſe (becauſe no man is born an *Artiſt* nor an *Angler*) I thought fit to give thee this notice. I might ſay more, but it is not fit for this place; but if this Diſcourſe which follows ſhall come to a ſecond impreſſion, which is poſſible, for ſlight books have been in this Age obſerved to have that fortune; I ſhall then for thy ſake be glad to correct what is faulty, or by a conference with any to explain or enlarge what is defective: but for this time I have neither
a wil-

To the Reader.

a willingneſs nor leaſure to ſay more, then wiſh thee a *rainy evening* to read this book in, and *that the eaſt wind may never blow when thou goeſt a fiſh-ng.* Farewel.

Iz. Wa.

BEcaufe in this Difcourfe of *Fifh* and *Fifhing* I have not obferved a method, which (though the Difcourfe be not long) may be fome inconvenience to the Reader, I have therefore for his eafier finding out fome particular things which are fpoken of, made this following Table.

and

The Table.

These directions the Reader may take as an ease in his search after some particular Fish, and the baits proper for them; and he will shew himselfe courteous in mending or passing by some errors in the Printer, which are not so many but that they may be pardoned.

The

The Complete
ANGLER.
OR,
The contemplative Mans
RECREATION.

$$\begin{cases} \text{PISCATOR.} \\ \text{VIATOR.} \end{cases}$$

Piscator.

Ou are wel over-
taken Sir; a good
morning to you;
I have ſtretch'd
my legs up *Tot-
nam Hil* to over-
take you, hoping
B   your

your bufineffe may occafion you towards *Ware*, this fine pleafant frefh *May day* in the Morning.

Viator. Sir, I fhall almoft anfwer your hopes: for my purpofe is to be at *Hodfden* (three miles fhort of that Town) I wil not fay, before I drink; but before I break my faft: for I have appointed a friend or two to meet me there at the *thatcht houfe*, about nine of the clock this morning; and that made me fo early up, and indeed, to walk fo faft.

Pifc. Sir, I know the *thatcht houfe* very well: I often make it my refting place, and tafte a cup of Ale there, for which liquor that place is very remarkable; and to that houfe I fhall by your favour accompany you, and either abate of my pace, or mend it, to enjoy fuch a companion as you feem to be, knowing that (as the Italians fay) *Good company makes the way feem fhorter.*

Viat. It may do fc Sir, with the
help

help of good difcourfe, which (me thinks) I may promife from you, that both look and fpeak fo chearfully. And to invite you to it, I do here promife you, that for my part, I will be as free and open-hearted, as difcretion will warrant me to be with a ftranger.

Pifc. Sir, I am right glad of your anfwer; and in confidence that you fpeak the truth, I fhall (Sir) put on a boldneffe to ask, whether pleafure or bufineffe has occafioned your Journey.

Viat. Indeed , Sir, a little bufineffe, and more pleafure : for my purpofe is to beftow a day or two in hunting the *Otter* (which my friend that I go to meet, tells me is more pleafant then any hunting whatfoever :) and having difpatcht a little bufineffe this day, my purpofe is to morrow to follow a pack of dogs of honeft Mr. —— ——, who hath appointed me and my friend to meet him upon *Amwel hill* to morrow morning by day break.

Pifc. Sir, my fortune hath anfwered my defires; and my purpofe is to beftow a day or two in helping to deftroy fome of thofe villanous vermin: for I hate them perfectly, becaufe they love fifh fo well, or rather, becaufe they deftroy fo much: indeed, fo much, that in my judgment, all men that keep Otter dogs ought to have a Penfion from the Commonwealth to incourage them to deftroy the very breed of thofe bafe *Otters*, they do fo much mifchief.

Viat. But what fay you to the *Foxes* of this Nation? would not you as willingly have them deftroyed? for doubtleffe they do as much mifchief as the *Otters*.

Pifc. Oh Sir, if they do, it is not fo much to me and my Fraternitie, as that bafe Vermin the *Otters* do.

Viat. Why Sir, I pray, of what
Fra-

Fraternity are you, that you are so angry with the poor *Otter?*

Pif. I am a Brother of the *Angle*, and therefore an enemy to the *Otter*, he does me and my friends so much mifchief;for you are to know, that we *Anglers* all love one another : and therefore do I hate the *Otter* perfectly, even for their fakes that are of my Brotherhood.

Viat. Sir, to be plain with you, I am forry you are an *Angler :* for I have heard many grave , ferious men pitie, and many pleafant men fcoffe at *Anglers.*

Pifc. Sir, There are many men that are by others taken to be ferious grave men, which we contemn and pitie; men of fowre complexions; mony-getting-men, that fpend all their time firft in getting, and next in anxious care to keep it: men that are condemn'd to be rich, and alwayes difcontented, or bufie. For thefe poor-rich-men , wee Anglers

pitie

pitie them; and ſtand in no need to
borrow their thoughts to think our
ſelves happie : For (truſt me, Sir)
we enjoy a contentedneſſe above the
reach of ſuch diſpoſitions.

And as for any ſcoffer, *qui moc-
kat mockabitur.* Let mee tell you,
(that you may tell him) what the
wittie French-man ſayes in ſuch a
Caſe. *When my* Cat *and I enter-
taine each other with mutuall apiſh
tricks (as playing with a garter,) who
knows but that I make her more ſport
then ſhe makes me? Shall I conclude
her ſimple, that has her time to begin
or refuſe ſportiveneſſe as freely as I
my ſelf have? Nay, who knows but
that our agreeing no better, is the de-
feɛt of my not underſtanding her language? (for doubtleſſe Cats talk and
reaſon with one another) and that ſhee
laughs at, and cenſures my folly, for
making her ſport, and pities mee for
underſtanding her no better?* To this
purpoſe ſpeaks *Mountagne* concerning

*The Lord
Mountagne
in his Apol.
for Ra-Se-
bond.*

ning *Cats:* And I hope I may take as great a libertie to blame any Scoffer, that has never heard what an Angler can fay in the justification of his Art and Pleasure.

But, if this satisfie not, I pray bid the Scoffer put this Epigram into his pocket, and read it every morning for his breakfast (for I wish him no better;) Hee shall finde it fix'd before the Dialogues of *Lucian* (who may be justly accounted the father of the Family of all *Scoffers:*) And though I owe none of that Fraternitie so much as good will, yet I have taken a little pleasant pains to make such a conversion of it as may make it the fitter for all of that Fraternity.

Lucian *well skill'd in* scoffing, *this has writ,*
Friend, that's your folly which you think your wit:
This you vent oft, void both of wit *and* fear,
Meaning an other, when your self you jeer.

But no more of the *Scoffer*; for
fince *Solomon* fayes, he is an abo-
mination to men, he fhall be fo to
me; and I think, to all that love
Vertue and *Angling.*

Viat. Sir, you have almoft ama-
Pro. 24. 9. zed me: for though I am no Scoffer, yet I have (I pray let me fpeak
it without offence) alwayes look'd
upon *Anglers* as more patient, and
more fimple men, then (I fear) I fhall
finde you to be.

Pifcat. Sir, I hope you will not
judge my earneftneffe to be impa-
tience: and for my *fimplicitie*, if
by that you mean a *harmlefneffe*, or
that *fimplicity* that was ufually found
in the Primitive Chriftians, who
were (as moft *Anglers* are) quiet
men, and followed peace; men that
were too wife to fell their confci-
ences to buy riches for vexation, and
a fear to die. Men that lived in
thofe times when there were fewer
Lawyers; for then a Lordfhip might
have

have been fafely conveyed in a
piece of Parchment no bigger then
your hand, though feveral skins are
not fufficient to do it in this wifer
Age. I fay, Sir, if you take us Anglers to be fuch fimple men as I have
fpoken of, then both my felf, and
thofe of my profeffion will be glad
to be fo underftood. But if by fimplicitie you meant to expreffe any
general defect in the underftanding
of thofe that profeffe and practife
Angling, I hope to make it appear
to you, that there is fo much contrary reafon (if you have but the patience to hear it) as may remove all
the anticipations that Time or Difcourfe may have poffeff'd you with,
againft that Ancient and laudable
Art.

Viat. Why (Sir) is Angling of
Antiquitie, and an Art, and an art
not eafily learn'd ?

Pifc. Yes (Sir:) and I doubt not
but that if you and I were to con-
verfe

verfe together but til night, I fhould leave you poffeff'd with the fame happie thoughts that now poffeffe me; not onely for the Antiquitie of it, but that it deferves commendations; and that 'tis an Art; and worthy the knowledge and practice of a wife, and a ferious man.

Viat. Sir, I pray fpeak of them what you fhall think fit; for wee have yet five miles to walk before wee fhall come to the *Thatcht houfe*. And, Sir, though my infirmities are many, yet I dare promife you, that both my patience and attention will indure to hear what you will fay till wee come thither: and if you pleafe to begin in order with the antiquity, when that is done, you fhall not want my attention to the commendations and accommodations of it: and laftly, if you fhall convince me that 'tis an Art, and an Art worth learning

ing, I fhall beg I may become your Scholer, both to wait upon you, and to be inftructed in the Art it elf.

Pifc. Oh Sir, 'tis not to be queftioned, but that it is an art, and an art worth your Learning: the queftion wil rather be, whether you be capable of learning it? For he that learns it, muft not onely bring an enquiring, fearching, and difcerning wit; but he muft bring alfo that *patience* you talk of, and a love and propenfity to the art it felf: but having once got and practifed it, then doubt not but the Art will (both for the pleafure and profit of it) prove like to *Vertue, a reward to it felf.*

Viat. Sir, I am now become fo ful of expectation, that I long much to have you proceed in your difcourfe: And firft, I pray Sir, let me hear concerning the antiquity of it.

Pifc.

Pifc. Sir, I wil preface no longer, but proceed in order as you defire me: And firft for the Antiquity of *Angling*, I fhall not fay much; but onely this; Some fay, it is as ancient as *Deucalions* Floud: and others (which I like better) fay, that *Belus* (who was the inventer of godly and vertuous Recreations) was the Inventer of it: and fome others fay, (for former times have had their Difquifitions about it) that *Seth*, one of the fons of *Adam*, taught it to his fons, and that by them it was derived to Pofterity. Others fay, that he left it engraven on thofe Pillars which hee erected to preferve the knowledg of the *Mathematicks*, *Mufick*, and the reft of thofe precious Arts, which by Gods appointment or allowance, and his noble induftry were thereby preferved from perifhing in *Noah's* Floud.

Thefe (my worthy Friend) have been the opinions of fome men, that pof-

J. Da.

Jer. Mar

possibly may have endeavoured to make it more ancient then may well be warranted. But for my part, I shall content my self in telling you, That *Angling* is much more ancient then the incarnation of our Saviour: For both in the Prophet *Amos*, and before him in *Job*, (which last Book is judged to be written by *Moses*) mention is made of *fish-hooks*, which must imply *Anglers* in those times.

Chap. 4. 2.

Chap. 41.

But (my worthy friend) as I would rather prove my self to be a Gentleman, by being *learned* and *humble*, *valiant* and *inoffensive*, *vertuous* and *communicable*, then by a fond ostentation of *riches*; or (wanting these Vertues my self) boast that these were in my Ancestors; [And yet I confesse, that where a noble and ancient Descent and such Merits meet in any man, it is a double dignification of that person:] and so, if this Antiquitie of Angling (which, for my part , I have not forc'd) shall.

like

like an ancient Familie, by either an honour, or an ornament to this vertuous Art which I both love and practise, I shall be the gladder that I made an accidental mention of it; and shall proceed to the justification, or rather commendation of it.

Viat. My worthy Friend, I am much pleased with your discourse, for that you seem to be so ingenuous, and so modest, as not to stretch arguments into Hyperbolicall expreſſions, but such as indeed they will reasonably bear; and I pray, proceed to the justification, or commendations of Angling, which I also long to hear from you.

Pisc. Sir, I shall proceed; and my next discourse shall be rather a Commendation, then a Justification of Angling: for, in my judgment, if it deserves to be commended, it is more then justified; for some practices that may be justified, deserve no commendation : yet there are none that deferve commendation but may be juftified.

And now having faid this much by way of preparation, I am next to tell you, that in ancient times a debate hath rifen, (and it is not yet refolved) Whether *Contemplation* or *Action* be the chiefeft thing wherin the happinefs of a man doth moft confift in this world?

Concerning which, fome have maintained their opinion of the firft, by faying, "[That the nearer we "Mortals come to God by way of "imitation, the more happy we "are:] And that God injoyes himfelf only by *Contemplation* of his own *Goodnefs*, *Eternity*, *Infinitenefs*, and *Power*, and the like; and upon this ground many of them prefer *Contemplation* before *Action* : and indeed, many of the Fathers feem to approve this opinion, as may appear in their Comments upon the words of our Saviour to * *Martha*.

* Luk. 10. 41,42.

And

And contrary to thefe, others of equal Authority and credit, have preferred *Action* to be chief; as experiments in *Phyfick*, and the application of it, both for the eafe and prolongation of mans life, by which man is enabled to act, and to do good to others: And they fay alfo, That *Action* is not only Doctrinal, but a maintainer of humane Society; and for thefe, and other reafons, to be preferr'd before *Contemplation.*

Concerning which two opinions, I fhall forbear to add a third, by declaring my own, and reft my felf contented in telling you (my worthy friend) that both thefe meet together, and do moft properly belong to the moft honeft, ingenious, harmlefs Art of Angling.

And firft I fhall tel you what fome have obferved, and I have found in my felf, That the very fitting by the Rivers fide, is not only the fitteft

place

place for, but will invite the Angler
to Contemplation: That it is the fit
teft place, feems to be witneffed by
the children of *Ifrael**, who having
banifh'd all mirth and Mufick from
their penfive hearts, and having
hung up their then mute Inftruments
upon the Willow trees, growing by
the Rivers of *Babylon,* fate down
upon thofe banks bemoaning the
ruines of *Sion,* and contemplating
their own fad condition,

Pfal. 137.

And an ingenuous *Spaniard* fayes,
"[That both Rivers, and the inha-
" bitants of the watery Element,
" were created for wife men to con-
" template, and fools to pafs by
" without confideration. And
though I am too wife to rank my
felf in the firft number, yet give me
leave to free my felf from the laft, by
offering to thee a fhort contemplation, firft of Rivers, and then of
Fifh : concerning which, I doubt
not but to relate to you many

C   things

things very confiderable.

Concerning Rivers, there be divers wonders reported of them by Authors, of fuch credit, that we need not deny them an Hiftorical faith.

As of a River in *Epirus*, that puts out any lighted Torch, and kindles any Torch that was not lighted. Of the River *Selarus*, that in a few hours turns a rod or a wand into ftone (and our *Camden* mentions the like wonder in *England*:) that there is a River in *Arabia*, of which all the Sheep that drink thereof have their Wool turned into a Vermilion colour. And one of no lefs credit then *Ariftotle*, tels us of a merry River, the River *Elufina*, that dances at the noife of Mufick, that with Mufick it bubbles, dances, and growes fandy, but returns to a wonted calmnefs and clearnefs when the Mufick ceafes. And laftly, (for I would not tire your patience) *Jofe-*

phus

In his *Wonders of nature.*

This is confirmed by *Ennius* and *Solon* in his holy Hiftory.

phus, that learned *Jew*, tells us of a River in *Judea*, that runs and moves swiftly all the six dayes of the week, and stands still and rests upon their *Sabbath* day. But Sir, left this difcourfe may feem tedious, I shall give it a fweet conclufion out of that holy Poet Mr. *George Herbert* his Divine Contemplation on Gods providence.

Lord, who hath praife enough, nay, who hath any?
None can exprefs thy works, but he that knows them:
And none can know thy works, they are fo many,
And fo complete, but only he that owes them.

We all acknowledge both thy power and love
To be exact, tranfcendent, and divine;
Who does fo ftrangely, and fo fweetly move,
Whilft all things have their end, yet none but thine.

Wherefore, moft Sacred Spirit, I here prefent
For me, and all my fellows praife to thee:
And juft it is that I fhould pay the rent,
Becaufe the benefit accrues to me.

And as concerning Fifh, in that Pfal. 104.

Pfalm

Pſal. 104. Pſalm, wherein, for height of Poetry and Wonders, the Prophet *David* ſeems even to exceed himſelf; how doth he there expreſs himſelfe in choice Metaphors, even to the amazement of a contemplative Reader, concerning the Sea, the Rivers, and the Fiſh therein contained. And the great Naturalliſt *Pliny* ſayes, "[That Natures great and wonder-"ful power is more demonſtrated in "the Sea, then on the Land.] And this may appear by the numerous and various Creatures, inhabiting both in and about that Element: as to the Readers of *Geſner, Randelitius, Pliny, Ariſtotle,* and others is demonſtrated: But I will ſweeten this diſcourſe alſo out of a contem-

Dubartas in the fifth day. plation in Divine *Dubartas,* who ſayes,

God quickened in the Sea and in the Rivers,
So many fiſhes of ſo many features,
That in the waters we may ſee all Creatures;

Even

Even all that on the earth is to be found,
As if the world were in deep waters drownd.
For seas(as well as Skies)have Sun,Moon,Stars;
(As wel as air)Swallows Rocks, and Stares;
(As wel as earth)Vines,Roses,Nettles,Melons,
Mushrooms,Pinks,Gilliflowers and many milions
Of other plants, more rare, more strange then
As very fishes living in the seas;   (these;
And also Rams,Calves,Horses,Hares and Hogs,
Wolves, Urchins, Lions, Elephants and Dogs;
Yea,Men and Maids, and which I most admire,
The Mitred Bishop, and the cowled Fryer.
Of which examples but a few years since,
Were shewn the Norway *and* Polonian *Prince.*

Thefe feem to be wonders, but
have had fo many confirmations
from men of Learning and credit,
that you need not doubt them; nor
are the number, nor the various
fhapes of fifhes, more ftrange or
more fit for *contemplation*, then their
different natures, inclinations and a-
&tions: concerning which I fhall beg
your patient ear a little longer.

The *Cuttle-fish* wil caſt a long gut out of her throat, which (like as an Angler does his line) ſhe ſendeth forth and pulleth in again at her pleaſure, according as ſhe ſees ſome little fiſh come neer to her; and the *Cuttle-fiſh* (being then hid in the gravel) lets the ſmaller fiſh nibble and bite the end of it; at which time ſhee by little and little draws the ſmaller fiſh ſo neer to her, that ſhe may leap upon her, and then catches and devours her: and for this reaſon ſome have called this fiſh the *Sea-Angler.*

Mount El-ſayes : and others affirm this.

There are alſo luſtful and chaſte fiſhes, of which I ſhall alſo give you examples.

And firſt, what *Dubartas* ſayes of a fiſh called the *Sargus*; which (becauſe none can expreſs it better then he does) I ſhall give you in his own words, ſuppoſing it ſhall not have the leſs credit for being Verſe, for he hath gathered this, and other obſervaobfervations out of Authors that have been great and induſtrious fearchers into the fecrets of nature.

The Adulterous Sargus *doth not only change,*
Wives everyday in the deep ſtreams, but (ſtrange
As if the honey of Sea-love delight
Could not ſuffice his ranging appetite,
Goes courting She-Goats *on the graſsie ſhore*
Horning their husbands that had horns before

And the fame Author writes concerning the *Cantharus*, that which you ſhall alſo heare in his own words.

But contrary, the conſtant Cantharus,
Is ever conſtant to his faithful Spouſe.
In nuptial duties ſpending his chaſte life,
Never loves any but his own dear wife.

Sir, but a little longer, and I have done.

Viat. Sir, take what liberty you think fit, for your diſcourſe ſeems to be Mufick, and charms me into an attention.

Pifc. Why then Sir, I will take a little libertie to tell, or rather to remember you what is faid of *Turtle Doves:* Firft, that they filently plight their troth and marry; and that then, the Survivor fcorns (as the *Thracian* women are faid to do) to out-live his or her Mate; and this is taken for fuch a truth, that if the Survivor fhall ever couple with another, the he or fhe, not only the living, but the dead, is denyed the *name* and *honour* of a true *Turtle Dove*.

And to parallel this Land Variety & teach mankind moral faithfulnefs & to condemn thofe that talk of Religion, and yet come fhort of the moral faith of fifh and fowl; Men that vi-olate the Law, affirm'd by Saint *Pau* to be writ in their hearts, and which he fayes fhal at the laft day condemn and leave them without excufe. I

Rom. 2.14
15.

pray

pray hearken to what *Dubartas* sings (for the hearing of such conjugal faithfulness, will be Musick to all chaste ears) and therefore, I say, hearken to what *Dubartas* sings of the *Mullet*:

But for chaste love the Mullet *hath no peer,*
For, if the Fisher hath surprised her pheer,
As mad with wc. to shoare she followeth,
Prest to confort him both in life and death.

On the contrary, what shall I say of the *House-Cock*, which treads any Hen, and then (contrary to the *Swan*, the *Partridg*, and *Pigeon*) takes no care to hatch, to feed, or to cherish his own Brood, but is senseless though they perish.

And 'tis considerable, that the *Hen* (which because she also takes any *Cock*, expects it not) who is sure the Chickens be her own, hath by a moral impression her care, and affection to her own Broode, more
then

then doubled, even to such a height,
that our Saviour in expressing his
love to *Jerusalem*, quotes her for an
example of tender affection, as his
Father had done *Job* for a pattern of
patience.

Mat. 23 37

And to parallel this *Cock*, there be
divers fishes that cast their spawne
on flags or stones, and then leave it
uncovered and exposed to become a
prey, and be devoured by Vermine
or other fishes: but other fishes (as
namely the *Barbel*) take such care
for the preservation of their feed,
that (unlike to the *Cock* or the *Cuckoe*)
they mutually labour (both the
Spawner, and the Melter) to cover
their spawne with sand, or watch it,
or hide it in some secret place unfre-
quented by Vermine, or by any fish
but themselves.

Sir, these examples may, to you
and others, seem strange; but they
are testified, some by *Aristotle*, some
by *Pliny*, some by *Gesner*, and by
divers

divers others of credit, and are believed and known by divers, both of
wiſdom and experience, to be a
truth; and are (as I ſaid at the beginning) fit for the contemplation
of a moſt ſerious, and a moſt pious
man.

And that they be fit for the contemplation of the moſt prudent and
pious, and peaceable men, ſeems
to be teſtified by the practice of ſo
many devout and contemplative
men; as the Patriarks or Prophets
of old, and of the Apoſtles of our
Saviour in theſe later times , of
which twelve he choſe four that
were Fiſhermen:concerning which
choice ſome have made theſe Obſervations.

Firſt, That he never reproved
theſe for their Imployment or Cal-
ling, as he did the Scribes and the
Mony-Changers. And ſecondly,
That he found the hearts of ſuch
men, men that by nature were fitted
for

for contemplation and quietneſs;
men of mild, and ſweet, and peaceable ſpirits, (as indeed moſt Anglers
are) theſe men our bleſſed Saviour
(who is obſerved to love to plant
grace in good natures) though nothing be too hard for him, yet theſe
men he choſe to call from their irreprovable imployment, and gave
them grace to be his Diſciples and
to follow him.

And it is obſervable, that it was
our Saviours will that his four Fiſhermen Apoſtles ſhould have a
prioritie of nomination in the catalogue of his twelve Apoſtles , as
namely firſt, S. *Peter*, *Andrew*, *James*
Mat.10. and *John*, and then the reſt in their
order.

And it is yet more obſervable,
that when our bleſſed Saviour went
up into the Mount, at his Transfiguration, when he left the reſt of his
Diſciples and choſe onely three to
bear him company, that theſe three
were

were all Fisher-men.

And since I have your promise to
hear me with patience, I will take a
liberty to look back upon an observation that hath been made by an ingenuous and learned man, who observes that God hath been pleased to
allow those whom he himselfe hath
appointed, to write his holy will in
holy Writ, yet to express his will in
such Metaphors as their former affe-
ctions or practise had inclined them
to; and he brings *Solomon* for an example, who before his conversion
was remarkably amorous, and after
by Gods appointment, writ that The Can-
Love-Song betwixt God and his ticles.
Church.

And if this hold in reason (as I
see none to the contrary) then it may
be probably concluded, that *Moses*
(whom I told you before, writ the
book of *Job*) and the Prophet *Amos*
were both Anglers, for you shal in all
the old Testament, find fish-hooks
but

but twice mentioned; namely, by meek *Moses*, the friend of God; and by the humble Prophet *A-mos*.

Concerning which laft, namely, the Prophet *Amos*, I fhall make but this Obfervation, That he that fhall read the humble, lowly, plain ftile of that Prophet, and compare it with the high, glorious, eloquent ftile of the prophet *Ifaiah* (though they be both equally true) may eafily believe him to be a good natured, plaine Fifher-man.

Which I do the rather believe, by comparing the affectionate, lowly, humble epiftles of S. *Peter*, S. *James* and S. *John*, whom we know were Fifhers, with the glorious language and high Metaphors of S. *Paul*, who we know was not.

Let me give you the example or two men more, that have lived nearer to our own times: firft of *Doctor Nowel* fometimes Dean of S. *Paul's*,

in

(in which Church his Monument ſtands yet undefaced) a man that in the Reformation of Queen *Eliza-beth* (not that of *Henry the VIII.*) was ſo noted for his meek ſpirit, deep Learning, Prudence and Piety, that the then Parliament and Convoca-tion, both choſe, injoyned, and truſt-ed him to be the man to make a Ca-techiſm for publick uſe, ſuch a one as ſhould ſtand as a rule for faith and manners to their poſteritie : And the good man (though he was very learned, yet knowing that God leads us not to heaven by hard queſtions) made that good, plain, unperplext Catechiſm, that is printed with the old Service Book. I ſay, this good man was as dear a lover, and con-ſtant practicer of Angling, as any Age can produce; and his cuſtome was to ſpend (beſides his fixt hours of prayer (thoſe hours which by command of the Church were en-joined the old Clergy, and volunta-rily

rily dedicated to devotion by many Primitive Christians:) besides those hours, this good man was observed to spend, or if you will, to bestow a tenth part of his time in Angling; and also (for I have conversed with those which have conversed with him) to bestow a tenth part of his Revenue, and all his fish, amongst the poor that inhabited near to those Rivers in which it was caught, saying often, *That Charity gave life to Religion* : and at his return would praise God he had spent that day free from worldly trouble, both harmlessly and in a Recreation that became a Church-man.

My next and last example shall be that undervaluer of money, the late Provost of *Eaton Colledg*, Sir *Henry Wotton*, (a man with whom I have often fish'd and convers'd) a man whose forraign imployments in the service of this Nation, and whose experience, learning, wit and

cheer

cheerfulneſs, made his company to be eſteemed one of the delights of mankind; this man, whoſe very approbation of Angling were ſufficient to convince any modeſt Cenſurer of it, this man was alſo a moſt dear lover, and a frequent practicer of the Art of Angling, of which he would ſay, "['Twas an imploy"ment for his idle time, which was "not idly ſpent;] for Angling was after tedious ſtudy "[A reſt to his "mind, a cheerer of his ſpirits, a di"vertion of ſadneſs, a calmer of un"quiet thoughts, a Moderator of paſ"ſions, a procurer of contentedneſs, "and that it begot habits of peace "and patience in thoſe that profeſt "and practic'd it.

Sir, This was the ſaying of that Learned man; and I do eaſily believe that peace, and patience, and a calm content did cohabit in the cheerful heart of Sir *Henry Wotton,* becauſe I know, that when he was beyond feventy years of age he made this defcription of a part of the prefent pleafure that poffeft him, as he fate quietly in a Summers evening on a bank a fifhing; it is a defcription of the Spring, which becaufe it glides as foft and fweetly from his pen, as that River does now by which it was then made, I fhall repeat unto you.

This day dame Nature feem'd in love :
The luftie fap began to move ;
Frefh juice did ftir th' imbracing Vines,
And birds had drawn their Valentines.
The jealous Trout, *that low did lye,*
Rofe at a well diffembled flie ;
There ftood my friend with patient skill,
Attending of his trembling quil.
Already were the eaves poffeft
With the fwift Pilgrims dawbed neft :
The Groves already did rejoice,
In Philomels *triumphing voice :*
The fhowrs were fhort, the weather mild,
The morning frefh, the evening fmil'd.

Jone

Jone *takes her neat rubb'd pail, and now*
She trips to milk the fand-red Cow ;
Where, for fome fturdy foot-ball Swain,
Jone *ftrokes a* Sillibub *or twaine.*
The fields and gardens were befet
With Tulips, Crocus, Violet,
And now, though late, the modeft Rofe
Did more then half a blufh difclofe.
Thus all looks gay and full of chear
To welcome the new liveried year.

Thefe were the thoughts that then
poffeft the undifturbed mind of Sir
Henry Wotton. Will you hear the
wifh of another Angler, and the
commendation of his happy life, Jo. Da.
which he alfo fings in Verfe.

Let me live harmlefly, and near the brink
Of Trent *or* Avon *have a dwelling place,*
Where I may fee my quil *or* cork *down fink,*
With eager bit of Pearch, *or* Bleak, *or* Dace;
And on the world and my Creator think, (brace;
Whilft fome men ftrive, ill gotten goods t' im—

And others spend their time in base excess
Of wine or worse,in war *and* wantonness.

Let them that list these pastimes still pursue,
And on such pleasing fancies feed their fill,
So I the fields *and* meadows *green may view,*
And daily by fresh Rivers *walk at will,*
Among the Daisies *and the* Violets *blue,*
Red Hyacinth,*and yellow* Daffadil,
　　Purple Narcissus,*like the morning rayes,*
　　Pale ganderglass *and azure* Culverkayes.

I count it higher pleasure to behold
The stately compass of the lofty Skie,
And in the midst thereof (like burning Gola)
The flaming Chariot of the worlds great eye,
The watry clouds, that in the aire up rold,
With sundry kinds of painted colours flye ;
　　And fair Aurora *lifting up her head,*
　　Still blushing,rise from old Tithonius *bed.*

The hils *and* mountains *raised from the* plains,
The plains *extended level with the* ground,
The grounds *divided into sundry* vains,
The vains *inclos'd with* rivers *running round ;*
　　　　　　　　　　　　　　These

These rivers making way through natures chains
With headlong course into the sea profound;
  The raging sea , beneath the vallies low,
  Where lakes, and rils, and rivulets do flow.

The loftie woods, the Forrests wide and long
Adorn'd with leaves & branches fresh & green,
In whose cool bowres the birds with many a song
Do welcom with their Quire the Sumers Queen:
The Meadows fair, where Flora's *gifts among*
Are intermixt, with verdant grass between.
  The silver-scaled fish that softly swim,
  Within the sweet brooks chrystal watry stream.

All these, and many more of his Creation,
That made the Heavens, the Angler oft doth see,
Taking therein no little delectation,
To think how strange, how wonderful they be ;
Framing thereof an inward contemplation,
To set his heart from other fancies free ;
  And whilst he looks on these with joyful eye,
  His mind is rapt above the Starry Skie.

Sir, I am glad my memory did
not lose these last Verses, because

they

they are fomewhat more pleafant and more futable to *May Day,* then my harfh Difcourfe, and I am glad your patience hath held out fo long, as to hear them and me; for both together have brought us within the fight of the *Thatcht Houfe*; and I muft be your Debtor (if you think it worth your attention) for the reft of my promifed difcourfe, till fome other opportunity and a like time of leifure.

Viat. Sir, You have Angled me on with much pleafure to the *thatcht Houfe,* and I now find your words true, *That good company makes the way feem fhort;* for, truft me, Sir, I thought we had wanted three miles of the *thatcht Houfe,* till you fhewed it me: but now we are at it, we'l turn into it, and refrefh our felves with a cup of Ale and a little reft.

Pifc. Moft gladly (Sir) and we'l drink a civil cup to all the *Otter Hun-*
ters

ters that are to meet you to morrow.

Viat. That we wil, Sir, and to all the lovers of Angling too, of which number, I am now one my felf, for by the help of your good dif-courfe and company, I have put on new thoughts both of the Art of An-gling, and of all that profefs it: and if you will but meet me too morrow at the time and place appointed, and beftow one day with me and my friends in hunting the *Otter*, I will the next two dayes wait upon you, and we two will for that time do no-thing but angle, and talk of fifh and fifhing.

Pifc. 'Tis a match, Sir, I'l not fail you, God willing, to be at *Amwel Hil* o morrow morning before Sun-rifing.

D 4   CHAP.

C H A P. II.

Viat. MY friend *Piscator*, you have kept time with my thoughts, for the Sun is just rising, and I my self just now come to this place, and the dogs have just now put down an *Otter*, look down at the bottom of the hil, there in that Meadow, chequered with water Lillies and Ladyfmocks, there you may fee what work they make: look, you fee all bufie, men and dogs, dogs and men, all bufie.

Pisc. Sir, I am right glad to meet you, and glad to have fo fair an entrance into this dayes fport, and glad to fee fo many dogs, and more men all in purfuit of the *Otter*; lets complement no longer, but joine unto them; come honeft *Viator*, lets

be

be gone, lets make hafte, I long to be doing; no reafonable hedge or ditch fhall hold me.

Viat. Gentleman Huntfman, where found you this *Otter*?

Hunt. Marry (Sir) we found her a mile off this place a fifhing; fhe has this morning eaten the greateft part of this *Trout*, fhe has only left thus much of it as you fee, and was fifhing for more; when we came we found her juft at it: but we were here very early, we were here an hour before Sun-rife, and have given her no reft fince we came: fure fhe'l hardly efcape all thefe dogs and men. I am to have the skin if we kill him.

Viat. Why, Sir, whats the skin worth?

Hunt. 'Tis worth ten fhillings to make gloves; the gloves of an *Otter* are the beft fortification for your hands againft wet weather that can be thought of.

Pifc. I

Pifc. I pray, honeſt Huntſman, let me ask you a pleaſant queſtion, Do you hunt a Beaſt or a fiſh?

H. Sir, It is not in my power to re-ſolve you; for the queſtion has been debated among many great Clerks, and they ſeem to differ about it; but moſt agree, that his tail is fiſh: and if his body be fiſh too, then I may ſay, that a fiſh will walk upon land (for an *Otter* does ſo) ſometimes five or ſix, or ten miles in a night. But (Sir) I can tell you certainly, that he devours much fiſh, and kils and ſpoils much more: And I can tell you, that he can ſmel a fiſh in the water one hundred yards from him (*Geſner* ſayes, much farther) and that his ſtones are good againſt the Falling-ſickneſs: and that there is an herb *Benione,* which being hung in a linen cloth near a Fiſh Pond, or any haunt that he uſes, makes him to avoid the place, which proves he can ſmell both by water and land.

And

And thus much for my knowledg of the *Otter*, which you may now fee above water at vent, and the dogs clofe with him; I now fee he will not laft long, follow therefore my Mafters, follow, for *Sweetlips* was like to have him at this vent.

via. Oh me, all the Horfe are got over the river, what fhall we do now?

Hun. Marry, ftay a little & follow, both they and the dogs will be fuddenly on this fide again, I warrant you, and the *Otter* too it may be: now have at him with *Kil buck*, for he vents again.

via. Marry fo he is, for look he vents in that corner. Now, now *Ringwood* has him. Come bring him to me. Look, 'tis a Bitch *Otter* upon my word, and fhe has lately whelped, lets go to the place where fhe was *put down*, and not far from it, you will find all her young ones, I dare warrant you: and kill them all too.

Hunt

Hunt. Come Gentlemen, come all, lets go to the place where we *put downe* the *Otter*; look you, hereabout it was that fhee kennell'd; look you, here it was indeed, for here's her young ones, no lefs then five: come lets kill them all.

Pifc. No, I pray Sir; fave me one, and I'll try if I can make her tame, as I know an ingenuous Gentleman in *Leicefter-fhire* has done; who hath not only made her tame, but to catch fifh, and doe many things of much pleafure.

Hunt. Take one with all my heart; but let us kill the reft. And now lets go to an honeft Alehoufe and fing *Old Rofe*, and rejoice all of us together.

Viat. Come my friend, let me invite you along with us; I'll bear your charges this night, and you fhall beare mine to morrow;

for

for my intention is to accompany you a day or two in fishing.

Pisc. Sir, your request is granted, and I shall be right glad, both to exchange such a courtesie, and also to enjoy your company.

Viat. Well, now lets go to your sport of Angling.

Pisc. Lets be going with all my heart, God keep you all, Gentlemen, and send you meet this day with another bitch *Otter*, and kill her merrily, and all her young ones too.

Viat. Now *Piscator*, where wil you begin to fish?

Pisc. We are not yet come to a likely place, I must walk a mile further yet before I begin.

Viat. Well then, I pray, as we walk, tell me freely how you like my Hoste, and the company? is not mine Hoste a witty man?

Pisc. Sir,

Pisc. Sir, To speak truly, he is not to me; for most of his conceits were either Scripture-jests, or lascivious jests; for which I count no man witty: for the Divel will help a man that way inclin'd, to the first, and his own corrupt nature (which he alwayes carries with him) to the latter. But a companion that feasts the company with *wit* and *mirth*, and leaves out the *sin* (which is usually mixt with them) he is the man: and indeed, such a man should have his charges born: and to such company I hope to bring you this night; for at *Trout-Hal*, not far from this place, where I purpose to lodg to night, there is usually an Angler that proves good company.

But for such discourse as we heard last night, it infects others; the very boyes will learn to talk and swear as they heard mine Host, and another of the company that shall be namelefs; well, you
know

know what example is able to do,
and I know what the Poet ſayes in
the like caſe :

—————*Many a one*
Owes to his Country his Religion :
And in another would as ſtrongly grow,
Had but his Nurſe or Mother taught him ſo.

This is reaſon put into Verſe, and
worthy the conſideration of a wiſe
man. But of this no more, for though
I love civility, yet I hate ſevere cenſures : I'll to my own Art, and I
doubt not but at yonder tree I ſhall
catch a *Chub*, and then we'll turn to
an honeſt cleanly Ale houſe that I
know right well, reſt our ſelves, and
dreſs it for our dinner.

via. Oh, Sir, a *Chub* is the worſt fiſh
that ſwims, I hoped for a *Trout* for
my dinner.

Piſ. Truſt me, Sir, there is not a likely place for a *Trout* hereabout, and
we ſtaid ſo long to take our leave of
                              your

your Huntſmen this morning, that the Sun is got ſo high, and ſhines ſo clear, that I will not undertake the catching of a *Trout* till evening; and though a *Chub* be by you and many others reckoned the worſt of all fiſh, yet you ſhall ſee I'll make it good fiſh by dreſſing it.

Viat. Why, how will you dreſs him?

Piſc. I'l tell you when I have caught him: look you here, Sir, do you ſee? (but you muſt ſtand very cloſe) there lye upon the top of the water twenty *Chubs*: I'll catch only one, and that ſhall be the biggeſt of them all: and that I will do ſo, I'll hold you twenty to one.

viat. I marry, Sir, now you talk like an Artiſt, and I'll ſay, you are one, when I ſhall ſee you perform what you ſay you can do; but I yet doubt it.

Piſc. And that you ſhall ſee me do preſently; look, the biggeſt of theſe
Chubs

Chubs has had fome bruife upon his tail, and that looks like a white fpot; that very *Chub* I mean to catch; fit you but down in the fhade, and ftay but a little while, and I'l warrant you I'l bring him to you.

viat. I'l fit down and hope well, becaufe you feem to be fo confident.

Pifc. Look you Sir, there he is, that very *Chub* that I fhewed you, with the white fpot on his tail; and I'l be as certain to make him a good difh of meat, as I was to catch him. I'l now lead you to an honeft Alehoufe, where we fhall find a cleanly room, Lavender in the windowes, and twenty Ballads ftuck about the wall; there my Hoftis (which I may tel you, is both cleanly and conveniently handfome(has dreft many a one for me, and fhall now drefs it after my fafhion, and I warrant it good meat.

viat. Come Sir, with all my heart,

E   for

for I begin to be hungry, and long to be at it, and indeed to reſt my ſelf too; for though I have walked but four miles this morning, yet I begin to be weary; yeſter dayes hunting hangs ſtil upon me.

Piſc. Wel Sir, and you ſhal quickly be at reſt, for yonder is the houſe I mean to bring you to.

Come Hoſtis, how do you ? wil you firſt give us a cup of your beſt Ale, and then dreſs this *Chub*, as you dreſt my laſt, when I and my friend were here about eight or ten daies ago? but you muſt do me one courteſie, it muſt be done inſtantly.

Hoſt. I wil do it, Mr. *Piſcator*, and with all the ſpeed I can.

Piſc. Now Sir, has not my Hoſtis made haſte ? and does not the fiſh look lovely ?

viat. Both, upon my word Sir, and therefore lets ſay Grace and fall to eating of it.

Piſc. Wel

Pisc. Well Sir, how do you like it?

viat. Truſt me,'tis as good meat as ever I taſted: now let me thank you for it, drink to you, and beg a courteſie of you; but it muſt not be deny'd me.

Pisc. What is it, I pray Sir? you are ſo modeſt, that me thinks I may promiſe to grant it before it is asked.

viat. Why Sir, it is that from henceforth you wil allow me to call you Maſter, and that really I may be your Scholer, for you are ſuch a companion, and have ſo quickly caught, and ſo excellently cook'd this fiſh, as makes me ambitious to be your ſcholer.

Pisc. Give me your hand: from this time forward I wil be your Maſter, and teach you as much of this Art as I am able; and will, as you deſire me, tel you ſomewhat of the nature of ſome of the fiſh which we

E 2   are

are to Angle for; and I am fure I fhal tel you more then every Angler yet knows.

And firft I will tel you how you fhall catch fuch a *Chub* as this was;& then how to cook him as this was: I could not have begun to teach you to catch any fifh more eafily then this fifh is caught; but then it muft be this particular way, and this you muft do:

Go to the fame hole, where in moft hot days you will finde floting neer the top of the water, at leaft a dozen or twenty *Chubs*; get a *Grafhopper* or two as you goe, and get fecretly behinde the tree, put it then upon your hook, and let your hook hang a quarter of a yard fhort of the top of the water, and 'tis very likely that the fhadow of your rod, which you muft reft on the tree, will caufe the *Chubs* to fink down to the bottom with fear; for they be a very fearful fifh, and the fhadow of a bird flying

flying over them will make them do so; but they will presently rise up to the top again, and there lie soaring till some shadow affrights them again : when they lie upon the top of the water, look out the best *Chub*, which you setting your self in a fit place, may very easily doe , and move your Rod as softly as a Snail moves, to that *Chub* you intend to catch; let your bait fall gently upon the water three or four inches before him, and he will infallibly take the bait, and you will be as sure to catch him; for hee is one of the leather-mouth'd fishes, of which a hook does scarce ever lose his hold : and therefore give him play enough before you offer to take him out of the water. Go your way presently, take my rod, and doe as I bid you, and I will sit down and mend my tackling till you return back.

viat. Truly, my loving Master, you have offered mee as fair as I could wifh: Ile goe and obferve your directions.

Look you, Mafter, what I have done; that which joyes my heart; caught juft fuch another *Chub* as yours was.

Pifc. Marry, and I am glad of it: I am like to have a towardly Scholer of you. I now fee, that with advice and practice you wil make an *Angler* in a fhort time.

Viat. But Mafter, What if I could not have found a *Grafhopper?*

Pif. Then I may tel you, that a *black Snail*, with his belly flit, to fhew his white; or a piece of foft *cheefe* wil ufually do as wel; nay, fometimes a *worm*, or any kind of *fly*; as the *Ant-fly*, the *Flefh-fly*, or *Wall-fly*, or the *Dor* or *Beetle*, (which you may find under a Cow-turd) or a *Bob*, which you wil find in the fame place, and in time wil be a *Beetle*; it is a fhort white worm, like to, and bigger then a Gentle; or a *Cod-worm*,

or

or *Cafe-worm*: any of thefe wil do ve-
-y wel to fifh in fuch a manner. And
after this manner you may catch a
Trout: in a hot evening, when as you
walk by a Brook, and fhal fee or
hear him leap at Flies, then if you
get a *Grafhopper* , put it on your
hook, with your line about two yards
long, ftanding behind a bufh or tree
where his hole is, and make your
bait ftir up and down on the top of
the water; you may, if you ftand
clofe, be fure of a bit, but not fure
to catch him, for he is not a leather
mouthed fifh: and after this manner
you may fifh for him with almoft a-
ny kind of live Flie, but efpecially with a *Grafhopper*.

Viat. But before you go further,
I pray good Mafter, what mean you
by a leather mouthed fifh.

Pifc. By a leather mouthed fifh,
I mean fuch as have their teeth in
their throat, as the *Chub* or *Cheven*,
and fo the *Barbel,* the *Gudgion* and

E 4 *Carp.*

Carp, and divers others have; and the hook being ftuck into the leather or skin of fuch fifh, does very feldome or never lofe its hold: But on the contrary, a *Pike,* a *Pearch,* or *Trout,* and fo fome other fifh, which have not their teeth in their throats, but in their mouthes, which you fhal obferve to be very full of bones, and the skin very thin, and little of it: I fay, of thefe fifh the hook never takes fo fure hold, but you often lofe the fifh unlefs he have gorg'd it.

Viat. I thank you good Mafter for this obfervation; but now what fhal be done with my *Chub* or *Cheven* that I have caught.

Pifc. Marry Sir, it fhall be given away to fome poor body, for Ile warrant you Ile give you a *Trout* for your fupper; and it is a good beginning of your Art to offer your firft fruits to the poor, who will both thank God and you for it.

And

And now lets walk towards the water again, and as I go Ile tel you when you catch your nex⁺ *Chub,* how to dreſſe it as this was.

viat. Come (good Maſter)I long to be going and learn your directi-on.

Piſc. You muſt dreſs it, or ſee it dreſt thus: When you have ſca-led him, waſh him very cleane, cut off his tail and fins; and waſh him not after you gut him, but chine or cut him through the middle as a ſalt fiſh is cut, then give him four or five ſcotches with your knife, broil him upon wood-cole or char-cole; but as he is broiling; baſte him of-ten with butter that ſhal be choice-ly good; and put good ſtore of ſalt into your butter, or ſalt him gently as you broil or baſte him; and bruiſe or cut very ſmal into your butter, a little Time, or ſome other ſweet herb that is in the Garden where you eat him: thus uſed, it takes a-
way

way the watrifh tafte which the *Chub*
or *Chevin* has,   and makes him a
choice difh of meat, as you your felf
know; for thus was that drefs'd,
which you did eat of to your dinner.

Or you may (for variety) drefs a
Chub another way, and you wil find
him very good, and his tongue and
head almoft as good as a Carps; but
then you muft be fure that no graffe
or weeds be left in his mouth or
throat.

Thus you muft drefs him : Slit
him through the middle,   then cut
him into four pieces; then put him
into a pewter difh,   and cover him
with another, put into him as much
White Wine as wil cover him, or
Spring water and Vinegar, and ftore
of Salt, with fome branches of
Time, and other fweet herbs; let
nim then be boiled gently over a
Chafing-difh with wood coles, and
when he is almoft boiled enough, put
half

half of the liquor from him, not the
top of it; put then into him a convenient quantity of the beſt butter
you can get, with a little Nutmeg
grated into it, and ſippets of white
bread: thus ordered, you wil find
the *Chevin* and the ſauce too, a
choice diſh of meat: And I have
been the more careful to give you a
perfect direction how to dreſs him,
becauſe he is a fiſh undervalued by
many, and I would gladly reſtore
him to ſome of his credit which he
has loſt by ill Cookery.

Viat. But Maſter, have you no
other way to catch a *Cheven*, or
Chub?

Piſc. Yes that I have, but I muſt
take time to tel it you hereafter; or
indeed, you muſt learn it by obſervation and practice, though this way
that I have taught you was the eaſi-
eſt to catch a *Chub*, at this time,
and at this place. And now weare
come again to the River; I wil (as
the

the Souldier ſayes) prepare for skir-
miſh; that is, draw out my Tackling, and try to catch a *Trout* for
ſupper.

Viat. Truſt me Maſter, I ſee now
it is a harder matter to catch a *Trout*
then a *Chub*; for I have put on patience, and followed you this two
hours, and not ſeen a fiſh ſtir, neither at your Minnow nor your
worm.

Piſc. Wel Scholer, you muſt
indure worſe luck ſometime, or you
will never make a good Angler. But
what ſay you now? there is a *Trout*
now, and a good one too, if I can
but hold him; and two or three
turns more will tire him: Now you
ſee he lies ſtill, and the ſleight is to
land him: Reach me that Landing
net: So (Sir) now he is mine own,
what ſay you? is not this worth all
my labour?

Viat. On my word Maſter,
this is a gallant *Trout*; what ſhall
we

we do with him?

Pifc. Marry ee'n eat him to fupper: We'l go to my Hoftis, from whence we came; fhe told me, as I was going out of door, that my brothet *Peter*, a good Angler, and a cheerful companion, had fent word he would lodg there to night, and bring a friend with him. My Hoftis has two beds, and I know you and I may have the beft: we'l rejoice with my brother *Peter* and his friend, tel tales, or fing Ballads, or make a Catch, or find fome harmlefs fport to content us.

Viat. A match, good Mafter, lets go to that houfe, for the linnen looks white, and fmels of Lavender, and I long to lye in a pair of fheets that fmels fo: lets be going, good Mafter, for I am hungry again with fifhing.

Pifc. Nay, ftay a little good Scholer, I caught my laft *Trout* with a worm, now I wil put on a Minow and

and try a quarter of an hour about
yonder trees for another, and ſo
walk towards our lodging. Loo k
you Scholer, thereabout we ſhall
have a bit preſently, or not at all:
Have with you (Sir!) on my word I
have him. Oh it is a great logger-
headed *Chub*: Come, hang him upon that Willow twig, and let's be
going. But turn out of the way a
little, good Scholer, towards yonder high hedg: We'l ſit whilſt this
ſhowr falls ſo gently upon the teem-
ing earth, and gives a ſweeter ſmel
to the lovely flowers that adorn
the verdant Meadows.

Look, under that broad *Beech tree*
I ſate down when I was laſt this way
a fiſhing, and the birds in the adjoin-
ing Grove ſeemed to have a friendly contention with an Echo, whoſe
dead voice ſeemed to live in a hollow cave. near to the brow of that
Primi oſe hil; there I ſate viewing the
Silver ſtreams glide ſilently towards
                                    their

their center, the tempeſtuous **Sea**, yet ſometimes oppoſed by rugged roots, and pibble ſtones, which broke their waves, and turned them into ſome: and ſometimes viewing the harmleſs Lambs, ſome leaping ſecurely in the cool ſhade, whilſt o-+hers ſported themſelvs in the cheerful Sun; and others were craving comfort from the ſwolne **U**dders of their bleating Dams. As I thus ſate, theſe and other ſighs had ſo fully poſſeſt my ſoul, that I thought as the Poet has happily expreſt it:

I was for that time lifted above earth;
And poſſeſt joyes not promiſ'd in my birth.

As I left this place, and entered into the next field, a ſecond pleaſure entertained me, 'twas a handſome Milk-maid, that had caſt away all care, and ſung like a *Nightingale*; her voice was good, and the Ditty fitted for it; 'twas that ſmooth Song which

which was made by *Kit Marlow*, now at leaft fifty years ago; and the Milk maids mother fung an anfwer to it, which was made by Sir *Walter Raleigh* in his younger dayes.

They were old fafhioned Poetry, but choicely good, I think much better then that now in fafhion in this Critical age. Look yonder, on my word, yonder they be both a milking again: I wil give her the *Chub*, and perfwade them to fing thofe two fongs to us.

Pifc. God fpeed, good woman, I have been a fifhing, and am going to *Bleak Hall* to my bed, and having caught more fifh then wil fup my felf and friend, wil beftow this upon you and your daughter, for I ufe to fel none.

Milkw. Marry God requite you Sir, and we'l eat it cheerfully: wil you drink a draught of red Cows milk?

Pifc. No, I thank you: but I pray do

d o us a courtefie that fhal ftand you
and your daughter in nothing, and
we wil think our felves ftil fomething
in your debt; it is but to fing us a
Song, that that was fung by you and
your daughter, when I laft paft over
this Meadow, about eight or nine
dayes fince.

Milk. what Song was it, I pray?
was it, *Come Shepherds deck your heads:*
or, *As at noon* Dulcina *refted*: or *Phi-
lida flouts me* ?

Pifc. No, it is none of thofe: it is a
Song that your daughter fung the
firft part, and you fung the anfwer to
it.

Milk. O I know it now, I learn'd
the firft part in my golden age, when
I was about the age of my daughter;
and the later part, which indeed fits
me beft, but two or three years ago;
you fhal, God willing , hear them
both. Come *Maudlin*, fing the firft
part to the Gentlemen with a merrie
heart, and Ile fing the fecond.

The

The Milk maids Song.

Come live with me, and be my Love,
And we wil all the pleasures prove
That vallies, Groves, or hils, or fields,
Or woods and steepie mountains yeelds.

Where we will sit upon the Rocks,
And see the Shepherds feed our flocks,
By shallow Rivers, *to whose falls*
Mellodious birds sing madrigals.

And I wil make thee beds of Roses,
And then a thousand fragrant posies,
A cap of flowers and a Kirtle,
Imbroidered all with leaves of Mirtle.

A Gown made of the finest wool
Which from our pretty Lambs we pull,
Slippers lin'd choicely for the cold,
With buckles of the purest gold.

A belt of straw and ivie buds,
With Coral clasps, and Amber studs :
And

And if these pleasures may thee move,
Come live with me, and be my Love.

The Shepherds Swains shal dance and sing
For thy delight each May morning :
If these delights thy mind may move,
Then live with me, and be my Love.

Via. Trust me Master, it is a choice
Song , and sweetly sung by honest
Maudlin : Ile bestow Sir *Thomas O-*
verbury's Milk maids wish upon her,
That she may dye in the Spring, and
have good store of flowers stuck round
about her winding sheet.

The Milk maids mothers answer.

If all the world and love were young,
And truth in every Shepherds tongue?
These pretty pleasures might me move,
To live with thee, and be thy love.

But time drives flocks from field to fold :
When rivers rage and rocks grow cold,

And

And Philomel *becometh dumb,*
The Reſt complains of cares to come.

The Flowers do fade, and wanton fields
To wayward Winter reckoning yeilds
A honey tongue, a heart of gall,
Is fancies ſpring, but ſorrows fall.

Thy gowns, thy ſhooes, thy beds of Roſes,
Thy Cap, thy Kirtle, and thy Poſies,
Soon break, ſoon wither, ſoon forgotten,
In folly ripe, in reaſon rotten.

Thy belt of ſtraw and Ivie buds,
Thy Coral claſps and Amber ſtuds,
All theſe in me no means can move
To come to thee, and be thy Love.

But could youth laſt, and love ſtil breea,
Had joyes no date, nor age no need;
Then thoſe delights my mind might
To live with thee, & be thy love. (move

Piſc. Wel ſung, good woman, I
thank you, I'l give you another diſh
                                        of

of fifh one of thefe dayes, and then beg another Song of you. Come Scholer, let *Maudlin* alone, do not you offer to fpoil her voice. Look, yonder comes my Hoftis to cal us to fupper. How now? is my brother *Peter* come?

Hoft. Yes, and a friend with him, they are both glad to hear you are in thefe parts, and long to fee you, and are hungry, and long to be at fupper.

F 3   CHAP.

C H A P. III.

Piscat. VVEL met bro-
ther *Peter*, I
heard   you
& a friend would lodg here to night,
and that has made me and my friend
cast to lodge here too ; my friend
is one that would faine be a brother
of the *Angle* : he has been an *Angler*
but this day, and I have taught him
how to catch a *Chub* with *daping* a
Grashopper, and he has caught a lusty
one of nineteen inches long.   But I
pray you brother, who is it that is
your companion ?

Peter. Brother *Piscator*, my friend
is an honest Country man, and his
name is *Coridon*, a most downright
witty merry companion that met me
here purposely to eat a *Trout* and be
pleasant, and I have not yet wet my
line

line fince I came from home: But I wil fit him to morrow with a *Trout* for his breakfaft, if the weather be any thing like.

Pifc. Nay brother, you fhall not delay him fo long, for look you here is a *Trout* will fill fix reafonable bellies. Come Hoftis, drefs it prefently, and get us what other meat the houfe wil afford, and give us fome good Ale, and lets be merrie.

The Defcription of a Trout.

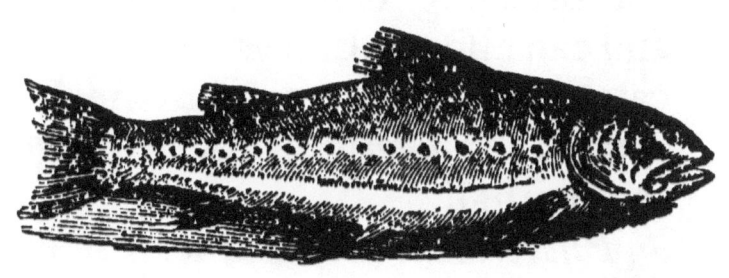

Peter

Peter. On my word, this *Trout* is in perfect feafon. Come, I thank you, and here's a hearty draught to you, and to all the brothers of the Angle, wherefoever they be, and to my young brothers good fortune to morrow; I wil furnifh him with a ʿod, if you wil furnifh him with the reft of the tackling, we wil fet him up and make him a fifher.

And I wil tel him one thing for his encouragement, that his fortune hath made him happy to be a Scho-ler to fuch a Mafter; a Mafter that knowes as much both of the nature and breeding of fifh, as any man; and can alfo tell him as well how to catch and cook them, from the *Mi-now* to the *Sammon*, as any that I ever met withall.

Pifc. Truft me, brother *Peter*, I find my Scholer to be fo futable to my own humour, which is to be free and pleafant, and civilly merry, that my refolution is to hide nothing from

from him. Believe me, Scholer, this is my refolution : and fo here's to you a hearty draught, and to all that love us, and the honeft Art of Angling.

Viat. Truft me, good Mafter, you fhall not fow your feed in barren ground, for I hope to return you an increafe anfwerable to your hopes; but however, you fhal find me obedient, and thankful , and ferviceable to my beft abilitie.

Pifc. 'Tis enough, honeft Scholer, come lets to fupper. Come my friend *Coridon*, this *Trout* looks lovely, it was twenty two inches when it was taken, and the belly of it look'd fome part of it as yellow as a Marygold, and part of it as white as a Lily, and yet me thinks it looks better in this good fawce.

Coridon. Indeed, honeft friend, it looks well, and taftes well, I thank you for it, and fo does my friend *Peter*, or elfe he is to blame.

Pet. Yeͨ

Pet. Yes, and ſo I do, we all
thank you, and when we have ſupt,
I wil get my friend *Coridon* to ſing
you a Song, for requital.

Cor. I wil ſing a Song if any body wil ſing another; elſe, to be plain
with you, I wil ſing none: I am
none of thoſe that ſing for meat, but
for company; I ſay, 'Tis merry in
Hall when men ſing all.

Piſc. I'l promiſe you I'l ſing a
Song that was lately made at my re-
queſt by Mr. *William Baſſe*, one that
has made the choice Songs of the
Hunter in his carrere, and of *Tom of
Bedlam*, and many others of note;
and this that I wil ſing is in praiſe of
Angling.

Cor. And then mine ſhall be the
praiſe of a Country mans life:
What will the reſt ſing of?

Pet. I wil promiſe you I wil ſing
another Song in praiſe of Angling,
to-morrow night, for we wil not part
till then, but fiſh to morrow, and
ſup

fup together, and the next day every man leave fifhing, and fall to his bufinefs.

Viat. 'Tis a match, and I wil provide you a Song or a Ketch againft then too, that fhal give fome addition of mirth to the company; for we wil be merrie.

Pifc. 'Tis a match my mafters; lets ev'n fay Grace, and turn to the fire, drink the other cup to wet our whiftles, and fo fing away all fad thoughts.

Come on my mafters, who begins? I think it is beft to draw cuts and avoid contention.

Pet. It is a match. Look, the fhorteft Cut fals to *Coridon.*

Cor. Well then, I wil begin; for I hate contention.

CORIDONS Song.

Oh the fweet contentment
The country man doth find!

High

high trolollie loliloe
high trolollie lee,
That quiet contemplation
Poſſeſſeth all my mind :
   Then care away,
    and wend along with me.

For Courts are full of flattery,
As hath too oft heen tri'd ;
   high trolollie lollie loe
   high trolollie lee,
The City full of wantonneſs,
and both are full of pride :
   Then care away,
    and wend along with me.

But oh the honeſt country man
Speaks truly from his heart,
   high trolollie lollie loe
   high trolollie lee,
His pride is in his Tillage,
bis Horſes and his Cart :
   Then care away,
    and wend along with me.
                Our

Our clothing is good sheep skins
Gray russet for our wives,
   high trolollie lollie loe
   high trolollie lee.
'Tis warmth and not gay clothing
that doth prolong our lives :
   Then care away,
   and wend along with me.

The ploughman, though he labor hard,
Yet on the Holy-day,
   high trolollie lollie loe
   high trolollie lec,
No Emperor *so merrily*
does pass his time away :
   Then care away,
   and wend along with me.

To recompence our Tillage,
The Heavens *afford us showrs,*
   high trolollie lollie loe
   high trolollie lee,
And for our sweet refreshments
the earth affords us bowers :
   Then care away,&c.
                The

The Cuckoe *and the* Nightingale
full merrily do sing,
   high trolollie lollie loe
   high trolollie lee,
And with their pleasant roundelayes,
bid welcome to the Spring :
   Then care away,
   and wend along with me.

This is not half the happiness
the Country man injoyes ;
   high trolollie lollie loe
   high trolollie lee,
Though others think they have as much
yet he that says so lies :
   Then come away, turn
   County man with me.

Pisc. Well sung *Coridon,* this
Song was sung with mettle, and it
was choicely fitted to the occasion;
I shall love you for it as long as I
know you : I would you were a brother of the Angle, for a companion
that is cheerful and free from swear-
ing

ing and scurrilous discourse, is worth gold. I love such mirth as does not make friends ashamed to look upon one another next morning; nor men (that cannot wel bear it) to repent the money they spend when they be warmed with drink : and take this for a rule, you may pick out such times and such companies, that you may make your selves merrier for a little then a great deal of money; for *'Tis the company and not the charge that makes the feast* : and such a companion you prove, I thank you for it.

But I will not complement you out of the debt that I owe you, and therefore I will begin my Song, and wish it may be as well liked.

The ANGLERS Song.

As inward love breeds outward talk,
The Hound *some praise, and some the* Hawk,
Some

Some better pleas'd with private sport,
Use Tenis, some a Mistris court :
   But these delights I neither wish,
   Nor envy, while I freely fish.

Who hunts, doth oft in danger ride
Who hauks, lures oft both far & wide ;
Who uses games, may often prove
A loser ; but who fals in love,
   Is fettered in fond Cupids snare :
   My Angle breeds me no such care.

Of Recreation there is none
So free as fishing is alone ;
All other pastimes do no less
Then mind and body both possess ;
   My hand alone my work can do,
   So I can fish and study too.

I care not, I, to fish in seas,
Fresh rivers best my mind do please,
Whose sweet calm course I contemplate ;
And seek in life to imitate ;
   In civil bounds I fain would keep,
   And for my past offences weep.

                      And

And when the timerous Trout *I wait*
To take, and he devours my bait,
How poor a thing sometimes I find
Will captivate a greedy mind:
  And when none bite, I praise the wife ,
  Whom vain alurements ne're surprise.

But yet though while I fish, I fast,
I make good fortune my repast,
And thereunto my friend invite,
In whom I more then that delight :
  Who is more welcome to my dish,
  Then to my Angle was my fish.

As well content no prize to take
As use of taken prize to make ;
For so our Lord was pleased when
He Fishers made Fishers of men;
  Where(which is in no other game)
  A man may fish and praise his name.

The first men that our Saviour dear
Did chuse to wait upon him here,
Blest Fishers were; and fish the last
Food was, that he on earth did taste .

G

I there-

I therefore ſtrive to follow thoſe,
Whom he to follow him hath choſe.
W. B.

Cor. Well ſung brother, you have paid your debt in good coyn, we Anglers are all beholding to the good man that made this Song. Come Hoſtis, give us more Ale and lets drink to him.

And now lets everie one go to bed that we may riſe early; but firſt lets pay our Reckoning, for I wil have nothing to hinder me in the morning, for I will prevent the Sun-riſing.

Pet. A match: Come *Coridon,* you are to be my Bed-fellow: I know brother you and your Scholer wil lie together; but where ſhal we meet to morrow night? for my friend *Coridon* and I will go up the water towards *Ware.*

Piſc. And my Scholer and I vvill go down tovvards *Waltam.*

Cor.

Cor, Then lets meet here, for here are freſh ſheets that ſmel of Lavender, and, I am ſure, we cannot expect better meat and better uſage.

Pet. 'Tis a match. Good night to every body.

Piſc. And ſo ſay I.

Viat. And ſo ſay I.

Piſc. Good morrow good Hoſtis, I ſee my brother *Peter* is in bed ſtill; Come, give my Scholer and me a cup of Ale, and be ſure you get us a good diſh of meat againſt ſupper, for we ſhall come hither as hungry as *Hawks*. Come Scholer, lets be going.

Viat. Good Maſter, as we walk towards the water, wil you be pleaſed to make the way ſeeme ſhorter by telling me firſt the nature of the *Trout*, and then how to catch him.

Piſc. My honeſt Scholer, I wil do
it

it freely: The *Trout* (for which I love to angle above any fiſh) may be juſtly ſaid (as the ancient Poets ſay of Wine, and we Engliſh ſay of Venſon) to be a generous fiſh, be-cauſe he has his ſeaſons, a fiſh that comes in, and goes out with the *Stag* or *Buck*: and you are to ob-ſerve, that as there be ſome *barren Does*, that are good in Summer; ſo there be ſome *barren Trouts*, that are good in Winter; but there are not many that are ſo, for uſually they be in their perfection in the month of *May*, and decline with the *Buck*: Now you are to take notice, that in ſeveral Countries, as in *Germany* and in other parts compar'd to ours, they differ much in their bigneſs, ſhape, and other wayes, and ſo do *Trouts*; 'tis wel known that in the Lake *Lemon*, the Lake of *Geneva*, there are *Trouts* taken, of three Cubits long, as is affirmed by *Geſner*, a Writer of good credit: and *Mercator* ſayes,

the

the *Trouts* that are taken in the Lake of *Geneva*, are a great part of the Merchandize of that famous City. And you are further to know, that there be certaine waters that breed *Trouts* remarkable, both for their number and fmalnefs- I know a little Brook in *Kent* that breeds them to a number incredible, and you may take them twentie or fortie in an hour, but none greater then about the fize of a *Gudgion*. There are alfo in divers Rivers, efpecially that relate to, or be near to the Sea, (as *VVinchefter*, or the Thames about *VVindfor*) a little *Trout* called a *Samlet* or *Skegger Trout* (in both which places I have caught twentie or fortie at a ftanding) that will bite as faft and as freely as *Minnows*; thefe be by fome taken to be young *Salmons,* but in thofe waters they never grow to bee bigger then a *Herring.*

There is alfo in *Kent,* neer to *Canterbury,* a *Trout* (called there a

G 3 *For-*

Fordig Trout) a *Trout (*that bears
the name of the Town where 'tis u-
fually caught) that is accounted rare
meat, many of them near the bignefs of a *Salmon*, but knowne by
their different colour, and in their
beft feafon cut very white;and none
have been known to be caught with
an Angle, unlefs it were one that
was caught by honeft Sir *George Haftings*, an excellent Angler (and
now with God)and he has told me,he
thought that *Trout* bit not for hunger, but wantonnefs; and 'tis the
rather to be believed, becaufe both
he then, and many others before
him have been curious to fearch into
their bellies what the food was by
which they lived; and have found
out nothing by which they might fatisfie their curiofitie.

Concerning which you are to
take notice, that it is reported, there
is a fifh that hath not any mouth, but
lives by taking breath by the porinfs
of

of her gils, and feeds and is nourifh'd by no man knows what; and this may be believed of the *Fordig Trout*, which (as it is faid of the *Stork*, that he knowes his feafon, fo he) knows his times (I think almoft his day) of coming into that River out of the Sea, where he lives (and it is like feeds) nine months of the year, and about three in the River of *Fordig*.

And now for fome confirmation of this; you are to know, that this *Trout* is thought to eat nothing in the frefh water ; and it may be the better believed, becaufe it is well known, that *Swallowes*, which are not feen to flye in *England* for fix months in the year, but about *Michaelmas* leave us for a hotter cli-mate ; yet fome of them, that have been left behind their fellows, have been found (many thoufand at a time) in hollow trees, where they have been obferved to live and fleep

View Sir *Fra. Bacon* exper. 898.

F 4   out

See *Topsel*
of *Frogs.* out the whole winter without meat; and so *Albertus* observes that there is one kind of *Frog* that hath her mouth naturally shut up about the end of *August*, and that she lives so all the Winter, and though it be strange to some, yet it is known to too many amongst us to bee doubted.

And so much for these *Fordidg Trouts*, which never afford an *Angler* sport, but either live their time of being in the fresh water by their meat formerly gotten in the Sea, (not unlike the *Swallow* or *Frog*) or by the vertue of the fresh water only, as the *Camelion* is said to live by the air.

There is also in *Northumberland*, a *Trout*, called a *Bull Trout*, of a much greater length and bigneße then any in these Southern parts; and there is in many Rivers that relate to the Sea, *Salmon Trouts* as much different one from another, both in

shape

ſhape and in their ſpots, as we ſee
Sheep differ one from another in
their ſhape and bigneſs, and in the
fineſs of their wool: and certainly
as ſome Paſtures do breed larger
Sheep, ſo do ſome Rivers, by reaſon of the ground over which they
run, breed larger *Trouts* .

Now the next thing that I will
commend to your conſideration is,
That the *Trout* is of a more ſudden
growth then other fiſh: concerning
which you are alſo to take notice,
that he lives not ſo long as the *Pearch*
and divers other fiſhes do, as Sir
Francis Bacon hath obſerved in his
Hiſtory of life and death.

And next, you are to take notice,
that after hee is come to his full
growth, he declines in his bodie, but
keeps his bigneſs or thrives in his
head till his death. And you are to
know that he wil about (eſpecially
before) the time of his Spawning, get
almoſt miraculouſly through *Weires*
and

and *Floud-Gates* againſt the ſtream, even through ſuch high and ſwift places as is almoſt incredible. Next, that the *Trout* uſually Spawns about *October* or *November*, but in ſome Rivers a little ſooner or later; which is the more obſervable, becauſe moſt other fiſh Spawne in the Spring or Summer, when the Sun hath warmed both the earth and water, and made it fit for generation.

And next, you are to note, that till the Snn gets to ſuch a height as to warm the earth and the water, the *Trout* is ſick, and lean, and lowſie, and unwholſome: for you ſhall in winter find him to have a big head, and then to be lank, and thin, & lean; at which time many of them have ſticking on them Sugs, or *Trout* lice, which is a kind of a worm, in ſhape like a Clove or a Pin, with a big head, and ſticks cloſe to him and ſucks his moiſture; thoſe I think the *Trout* breeds himſelfe, and never

thrives

thrives til he free himfelf from them, which is till warm weather comes, and then as he growes ſtronger, he gets from the dead, ſtill water, into the ſharp ſtreames and the gravel, and there rubs off theſe worms or lice : and then as he grows ſtronger, ſo he gets him into ſwifter and ſwifter ſtreams, and there lies atthe watch for any flie or Minow that comes neer to him ; and he eſpecially loves the *May* flie, which is bred of the *Cod-worm* or *Caddis*; and theſe make the *Trout* bold and luſtie, and he is uſually fatter, and better meat at the end of that month, then at any time of the year.

Now you are to know, that it is obſerved, that uſually the beſt *Trouts* are either red or yellow, though ſome be white and yet good; but that is not uſual ; and it is a note obſervable that the female *Trout* hath uſually a leſs head and a deeper body then the male *Trout* ; and a little
head

head to any fish, either *Trout, Salmon,* or other fish, is a sign that that fish is in season.

But yet you are to note, that as you see some Willows or Palm trees bud and blossome sooner then others do, so some *Trouts* be in some Rivers sooner in season; and as the Holly or Oak are longer before they cast their Leaves, so are some *Trouts* in some Rivers longer before they go out of season.

CHAP.

CHAP. IV.

AND having told you thefe Obfervations concerning *Trouts*, I fhall next tell you how to catch them : which is ufually with a *Worm*, or a *Minnow* (which fome call a *Penke*;) or with a *Flie*, either a *natural* or an *artificial* Flie: Concerning which three I wil give you fome Obfervations and Directions.

For Worms, there be very many forts; fome bred onely in the earth, as the *earth worm* ; others amongft or of plants, as the *dug worm* ; and others in the bodies of living creatures ; or fome of dead flefh, as the *Magot* or *Gentle*, and others.

Now thefe be moft of them particularly good for particular fifhes: but for the *Trout* the *dew - worm,*
which

(which some also cal the *Lob-worm*) and the *Brandling* are the chief; and especially the first for a great Trout, and the later for a lesse.   There be also of *lob-worms*, some called *squirel-tails* (a worm which has a red head, a streak down the back, and a broad tail) which are noted to be the best, because they are the toughest, and and most lively, and live longest in the water : for you are to know, that a dead worm is but a dead bait, and like to catch nothing, compared to a lively, quick, stirring worm : And for a *Brandling*, hee is usually found in an old dunghil, or some very rotten place neer to it ; but most usually in cow dung, or hogs dung, rather then horse dung, which is somewhat too hot and dry for that worm.

There are also divers other kindes of worms, which for colour and shape alter even as the ground out of which they are got: as the *marsh-worm,*

worm, the *tag-tail*, the *flag-worm*,
the *dock-worm*, the *oake-worm*, the
gilt-tail, and too many to name,
even as many forts, as fome think
there be of feverall kinds of birds in
the air: of which I fhall fay no
more, but tell you, that what worms
foever you fifh with, are the better
for being long kept before they be
ufed; and in cafe you have not been
fo provident, then the way to cleanfe
and fcoure them quickly, is to put
them all night in water, if they be
Lob-worms, and then put them into your bag with fennel: but you
muft not put your Brandling above
an hour in water, and then put them
into fennel for fudden ufe: but if
you have time, and purpofe to keep
them long, then they be beft preferved in an earthen pot with good
ftore of *moffe*, which is to be frefh
every week or eight dayes; or at
leaft taken from them, and clean
wafh'd, and wrung betwixt your
hands

hands till it be dry, and then put it to them again : And for Mofs you are to note, that there be divers kindes of it which I could name to you, but wil onely tel you, that that which is likeft a *Bucks horn* is the beft; except it be *white* Mofs, which grows on fome heaths, and is hard to be found.

For the *Minnow* or *Penke*, he is eafily found and caught in April, for then hee appears in the Rivers: but Nature hath taught him to fhelter and hide himfelf in the Winter in ditches that be neer to the River, and there both to hide and keep himfelf warm in the weeds, which rot not fo foon as in a running River ; in which place if hee were in Winter, the diftempered Floods that are ufually in that feafon, would fuffer him to have no reft, but carry him headlong to Mils and Weires to his confufion. And of thefe *Minnows*, firft you are to know, that

the

the biggeſt ſize is not the beſt ; and
next, that the middle ſize and the
whiteſt are the beſt : and then you
are to know , that I cannot well
teach in words, but muſt ſhew you
how to put it on your hook, that it
may turn the better : And you are
alſo to know, that it is impoſsible it
ſhould turn too quick : And you are
yet to know, that in caſe you want
a Minnow, then a ſmall *Loch*, or a
Sticklebag, or any other ſmall Fiſh
will ſerve as wel : And you are yet
to know, that you may ſalt, and by
that means keep them fit for uſe
three or four dayes or longer ; and
that of ſalt, bay ſalt is the beſt.

Now for *Flies*, which is the third
bait wherewith *Trouts* are uſually
taken. You are to know, that there
are as many ſorts of Flies as there be
of Fruits : I will name you but ſome
of them : as the *dun flie*, the *ſtone
flie*, the *red flie*, the *moor flie*, the
tawny flie, the *ſhel flie*, the *cloudy* or

black-

blackiſh *flie:* there be of Flies, *Ca-*
terpillars, and *Canker flies,* and *Bear*
flies; and indeed, too many either
for mee to name, or for you to remember: and their breeding is ſo
various and wonderful, that I might
eaſily amaze my ſelf, and tire you in
a relation of them.

And yet I wil exerciſe your promiſed patience by ſaying a little of
the *Caterpillar,* or the *Palmer flie* or
worm; that by them you may gueſs
what a work it were in a Diſcourſe
but to run over thoſe very many
flies, worms, and little living creatures with which the Sun and Summer adorn and beautifie the river
banks and meadows; both for the
recreation and contemplation of the
Angler: and which (I think) I my-
ſelf enjoy more then any other man
that is not of my profeſsion,

Pliny holds an opinion, that many have their birth or being from a
dew that in the Spring falls upon the
leaves

leaves of trees; and that fome kinds of them are from a dew left upon herbs or flowers: and others from a dew left upon Colworts or Cabbages: All which kindes of dews being thickened and condenfed, are by the Suns generative heat moft of them hatch'd, and in three dayes made living creatures, and of feveral fhapes and colours; fome being hard and tough, fome fmooth and foft; fome are horned in their head, fome in their tail, fome have none; fome have hair, fome none; fome have fixteen feet, fome lefs, and fome have none: but (as our *Topfel* hath with great diligence obferved) thofe which have none, move upon the earth, or upon broad leaves, their motion being not unlike to the waves of the fea. Some of them hee alfo obferves to be bred of the eggs of other Caterpillers: and that thofe in their time turn to be *Butter-flies*; and again, that their eggs turn the

In his Hi- ftory of Serpents.

H 2　　fol-

following yeer to be *Caterpillers*.

'Tis endleffe to tell you what the curious Searchers into Natures pro-ductions, have obferved of thefe Worms and Flies: But yet I fhall tell you what our *Topfel* fayes of the *Canker*, or *Palmer-worm*, or *Cater-piller*; That wheras others content themfelves to feed on particular herbs or leaves (for moft think, thofe very leaves that gave them life and fhape, give them a particular feed-ing and nourifhment, and that up-on them they ufually abide;) yet he obferves, that this is called a *Pil-grim* or *Palmer-worm*, for his very wandering life and various food; not contenting himfelf (as others do) with any certain place for his abode, nor any certain kinde of herb or flower for his feeding; but will boldly and diforderly wander up and down, and not endure to be kept to a diet, or fixt to a particular place.

Nay,

Nay, the very colours of *Caterpillers* are, as one has obſerved, very elegant and beautiful: I ſhal (for a taſte of the reſt (deſcribe one of them, which I will ſometime the next month, ſhew you feeding on a Willow tree, and you ſhal find him punctually to anſwer this very deſcription: "His "lips and mouth ſomewhat yel- "low, his eyes black as Jet, his "fore-head purple, his feet and "hinder parts green, his tail two "forked and black, the whole body "ſtain'd with a kind of red ſpots "which run along the neck and "ſhoulder-blades, not unlike the "form of a Croſs, or the letter X, "made thus croſs-wiſe, and a "white line drawn down his back "to his tail; all which add much "beauty to his whole body. And it is to me obſervable, that at a fix'd age this *Caterpiller* gives over to eat, and towards winter comes to be coverd over with a ſtrange ſhell or cruſt, and

H 3 ſo

ſo lives a kind of dead life, without eating all the winter, and (as others View Sir *Fra. Bacon* exper. 728 & 90. in his Natu-ral Hiſtory of ſeveral kinds turn to be ſeveral kinds of flies and vermin, the Spring following) ſo this *Caterpiller* then turns to be a painted Butterflye.

Come, come my Scholer, you ſee the River ſtops our morning walk, and I wil alſo here ſtop my diſcourſe, only as we ſit down under this Honey-Suckle hedge, whilſt I look a Line to fit the Rod that our brother *Peter* has lent you, I ſhall for a little confirmation of what I have ſaid, repeat the obſervation of the Lord *Bartas.*

God not contented to each kind to give,
And to infuſe the vertue generative,
By his wiſe power made many creatures breed
Of liveleſs bodies, without Venus *deed.*

So the cold humour breeds the Salamander,
Who (in effect) like to her birth commander,
                                    With

With child with hundred winters,with her touch
Quencheth the fire,though glowing ne'r fo much

So in the fire in burning furnace fprings
The fly Peraufta *with the flaming wings;*
Without the fire it dies, in it, it joyes,
Living in that which all things elfe deftroyes.

So flow Boötes *underneath him fees* Gerh.
*In th'icie Iflands*Goflings *hatcht of trees,* Herbal
Whofe fruitful leaves falling into the water, Cambden.
Are turn'd(tis' known) to living fowls foon after

So rotten planks of broken fhips, do change
To Barnacles.   *Oh transformation ftrange!*
'Twas firft a green tree,then a broken hull,
Lately a Mufhroom, now a flying Gull.

*Vi.*Oh my good Mafter,this morning walk has been fpent to my great
pleafure and wonder: but I pray,
when fhall I have your direction
how to make Artificial flyes, like to
thofe that the *Trout* loves beft? and
alfo how to ufe them?

H 4   *Pifc.*

Pisc. My honeſt Scholer, it is now paſt five of the Clock, we will fiſh til nine, and then go to Breakfaſt: Go you to yonder *Sycamore tree*, and hide your bottle of drink under the hollow root of it; for about that time, and in that place, we wil make a brave Breakfaſt with a piece of powdered Bief, and a Radiſh or two that I have in my Fiſh-bag; we ſhall, I warrant you, make a good honeſt, wholſome, hungry Breakfaſt, and I will give you direction for the making and uſing of your fly: and in the mean time, there is your Rod and line; and my advice is, that you fiſh as you ſee mee do, and lets try which can catch the firſt fiſh.

Viat. I thank you, Maſter, I will obſerve and practice your direction as far as I am able.

Pisc. Look you Scholer, you ſee I have hold of a good fiſh: I now ſee it is a *Trout*; I pray put that net under

under him, and touch not my line, for if you do, then wee break all. Well done, Scholer, I thank you. Now for an other. Truft me, I have another bite: Come Scholer, come lay down your Rod, and help me to land this as you did the other. So, now we fhall be fure to have a good difh of fifh for fupper.

Viat. I am glad of that, but I have no fortune; fure Mafter yours is a better Rod, and better Tackling.

Pifc. Nay then, take mine and I will fifh with yours. Look you, Scholer, I have another: come, do as you did before. And now I have a bite at another. Oh me he has broke all, there's half a line and a good hook loft.

Viat. Mafter, I can neither catch with the firft nor fecond Angle; I have no fortune.

Pifc. Look you, Scholer, I have yet another: and now having caught
three

three brace of *Trouts,* I will tel you a ſhort Tale as we walk towards our Breakfaſt. A Scholer (a Preacher I ſhould ſay) that was to preach to procure the approbation of a Pariſh, that he might be their Lecturer, had got from a fellow Pupil of his the Copy of a Sermon that was firſt preached with a great commendation by him that compoſed and precht it; and though the borrower of it preach't it word for word, as it was at firſt, yet it was utterly diſlik'd as it was preach'd by the ſecond; which the Sermon Borrower complained of to the Lender of it, and was thus anſwered; I lent you indeed my *Fiddle,* but not my *Fiddleſtick;* and you are to know, that every one cannot make muſick with my words which are fitted for my own mouth. And ſo my Scholer, you are to know, that as the ill pronunciation or ill accenting of a word in a Sermon ſpoiles it, ſo the ill carriage of

your

your Line, or not fiſhing even to a foot in a right place, makes you loſe your labour: and you are to know, that though you have my Fiddle, that is,my very Rod and Tacklings with which you ſee I catch fiſh, yet you have not my Fiddle ſtick, that is,skill to know how to carry your hand and line ; and this muſt be taught you(for you are to remember I told you Angling is an Art) either by practice,or a long obſervation,or both.

But now lets ſay Grace, and fall to Breakfaſt; what ſay you Scholer, to the providence of an old Angler? Does not this meat taſte well? and was not this place well choſen to eat it? for this *Sycamore* tree will ſhade us from the Suns heat.

Viat. All excellent good,Maſter, and my ſtomack excellent too ; I have been at many coſtly Dinners that have not afforded me half this content: and now good Maſter,to

your

your promifed direction for making and ordering my Artificiall flye.

Pifc. My honeft Scholer, I will do it, for it is a debt due unto you, by my promife: and becaufe you fhall not think your felf more engaged to me then indeed you really are, therefore I will tell you freely, I find Mr. *Thomas Barker* (a Gentleman that has fpent much time and money in Angling) deal fo judicially and freely in a little book of his of Angling, and efpecially of making and Angling with a *flye* for a *Trout*, that I will give you his very directions without much variation, which fhal follow.

Let your rod be light, and very gentle, I think the beft are of two pieces; the line fhould not exceed, efpecially for three or four links towards the hook) I fay, not exceed

ceed three or four haires; but if
you can attain to Angle with one
haire, you will have more rifes,
and catch more fifh. Now you
muft bee fure not to cumber your-
felfe with too long a Line, as moft
do: and before you begin to angle, caft to have the wind on your
back, and the Sun (if it fhines) to
be before you, and to fifh down
the ftreame) and carry the point
or top of the Rod downeward;
by which meanes the fhadow of
your felfe, and Rod too will be the
leaft offenfive to the Fifh, for the
fight of any fhadow amazes the
fifh, and fpoiles your fport, of
which you muft take a great
care.

In the middle of *March* (till
which time a man fhould not in
honeftie catch a *Trout*) or in *A-
pril*, if the weather be dark, or a little windy, or cloudie, the beft fifhing

is

is with the *Palmer-worm,* of which I laſt ſpoke to you; but of theſe there be divers kinds, or at leaſt of divers colours, theſe and the *May-fly* are the ground of all *fly-*Angling, which are to be thus made :

Firſt you muſt arm your hook, with the line in the inſide of it; then take your Sciſſers and cut ſo much of a browne *Malards* feather as in your own reaſon wil make the wings of it, you having withall regard to the bigneſs or littleneſs of your hook, then lay the outmoſt part of your feather next to your hook, then the point of your feather next the ſhank of your hook; and having ſo done, whip it three or four times about the hook with the ſame Silk, with which your hook was armed, and having made the Silk faſt, take the hackel of a *Cock* or *Capons* neck, or a *Plovers* top, which is uſually better; take off the one ſide of the feather, and then take the hackel, Silk

or

or Crewel, Gold or Silver thred, make thefe faft at the bent of the hook, that is to fay, below your arming) then you muft take the hackel, the filver or gold thred, and work it up to the wings, fhifting or ftil removing your fingers as you turn the Silk about the hook: and ftill looking at every ftop or turne that your gold, or what materials foever you make your *Fly* of, do lye right and neatly; and if you find they do fo, then when you have made the head, make all faft, and then work your hackel up to the head, and make that faft; and then with a needle or pin divide the wing into two, and then with the arming Silk whip it about crofs-wayes betwixt the wings, and then with your thumb you muft turn the point of the feather towards the bent of the hook, and then work three or four times about the fhank of the hook and then view the proportion, and if all be neat, and

to

to your liking, faften.

I confefs, no direction can be given to make a man of a dull capacity able to make a flye well; and yet I know, this, with a little practice, wil help and ingenuous Angler in a good degree; but to fee a fly made by another, is the beft teaching to make it, and then an ingenuous Angler may walk by the River and mark what fly falls on the water that day, and catch one of them, if he fee the *Trouts* leap at a fly of that kind, and having alwaies hooks ready hung with him, and having a bag alfo, alwaies with him with Bears hair, or the hair of a brown or fad coloured Heifer, hackels of a Cock or Capon, feveral coloured Silk and Crewel to make the body of the fly, the feathers of a Drakes he ad, black or brown fheeps wool, or Hogs wool, or hair, thred of Gold, and of filver; filk of feveral colours (efpecially fad coloured to make the head:) and there

there be alfo other colour'd feathers both of birds and of peckled fowl. I fay, having thofe with him in a bag, and trying to make a flie, though he mifs at firft, yet fhal he at laft hit it better, even to a perfection which none can well teach him; and if he hit to make his *flie* right, and have the luck to hit alfo where there is ftore of *trouts*, and a right wind, he fhall catch fuch ftore of them, as will encourage him to grow more and more in love with the Art of *flie-making*.

Viat. But my loving Mafter, if any wind will not ferve, then I wifh I were in *Lapland*, to buy a good wind of one of the honeft witches, that fell fo many winds, and fo cheap.

Pifc. Marry Scholer, but I would not be there, nor indeed from under this tree; for look how it begins to rain, and by the clouds (if I miftake not) we fhall prefently have a fmoa-

I   king

king ſhowre ; and therefore ſit cloſe,
this *Sycamore tree* will ſhelter us ; and
I will tell you, as they ſhall come into
my mind, more obſervations of flie-
fiſhing for a *Trout.*

But firſt, for the Winde ; you are
to take notice that of the windes the
South winde is ſaid to be beſt.   One
obſerves ,   That
         VVhen the winde is ſouth,
It blows your bait into a fiſhes mouth.

Next to that, the *weſt* winde is believed to be the beſt : and having
told you that the *Eaſt* winde is the
worſt,   I need not tell you which
winde is beſt in the third degree :
And yet (as *Solomon* obſerves, that
Hee that conſiders the winde ſhall ne-
ver ſow :   ſo hee that buſies his head
too much about them, (if the weather be not made extreme cold by
an Eaſt winde) ſhall be a little ſu-
perſtitious : for as it is obſerved by
ſome, That there is no good horſe
                                              of

of a bad colour; fo I have obferved, that if it be a clowdy day, and
not extreme cold, let the winde fit
in what corner it will, and do its
worft.   And yet take this for a
Rule, that I would willingly fifh
on the Lee-fhore: and you are to
take notice, that the Fifh lies, or
fwimms neerer the bottom in Winter then in Summer, and alfo neerer
the bottom in any cold day.

But I promifed to tell you more
of the Flie-fifhing for a *Trout,*(which
I may have time enough to do, for
you fee it rains *May-butter.*) Firft for
a *May-flie,* you may make his body
with greenifh coloured crewel, or
willow colour; darkning it in moft
places, with waxed filk, or rib d
with a black hare, or fome of them
rib'd with filver thred; and fuch
wings for the colour as you fee the
flie to have at that feafon;nay at that
very day on the water.   Or you may
make the *Oak-flie* with an Orange-
I 2   tawny

tawny and black ground, and the
brown of a Mallards feather for the
wings; and you are to know, that
thefe two are moft excellent *flies*, that
is, the *May-flie* and the *Oak-flie*:
And let me again tell you, that you
keep as far from the water as you can
pofsibly, whether you fifh with a flie
or worm, and fifh down the ftream;
and when you fifh with a flie, if it be
pofsible, let no part of your line
touch the water, but your flie only;
and be ftil moving your fly upon the
water, or cafting it into the water;
you your felf, being alfo alwaies moving down the ftream. M^r. *Barker*
commends feverall forts of the palmer flies, not only thofe rib'd with
filver and gold, but others that have
their bodies all made of black, or
fome with red, and a red hackel; you
may alfo make the *hawthorn-flie*,
which is all black and not big, but very fmal, the fmaller the better; or the
oak-fly, the body of which is Orange
colour

colour and black crewel, with a brown wing, or a *fly* made with a peacocks feather, is excellent in a bright day : you muſt be ſure you want not in your *Magazin* bag, the Peacocks feather, and grounds of ſuch wool, and crewel as will make the Graſshopper: and note, that uſually, the ſmalleſt flies are beſt; and note alſo, that, the light flie does uſually make moſt ſport in a dark day : and the darkeſt and leaſt flie in a bright or cleare day; and laſtly note, that you are to repaire upon any occaſion to your *Magazin bag*, and upon any occaſion vary and make them according to your fancy.

And now I ſhall tell you, that the fiſhing with a naturall flie is excellent, and affords much pleaſure; they may be found thus, the *May-fly* uſually in and about that month neer to the River ſide, eſpecially againſt rain ; the *Oak-fly* on the Butt or body of an *Oak* or *Aſh*, from the be-

I 3   ginning

ginning of *May* to the end of *August* it is a brownish fly, and easie to be so found, and stands usually with his head downward, that is to say, towards the root of the tree; the smal black fly, or *hawthorn* fly is to be had on any Hawthorn bush, after the leaves be come forth; with these and a short Line (as I shewed to Angle for a *Chub*) you may dap or dop, and also with a *Grashopper*, behind a tree, or in any deep hole, still making it to move on the top of the water, as if it were alive, and still keeping your self out of sight, you shall certainly have sport if there be *Trouts*; yea in a hot day, but especially in the evening of a hot day.

And now, Scholer, my direction for fly-fishing is ended with this showre, for it has done raining, and now look about you, and see how pleasantly that Meadow looks, nay and the earth smels as sweetly too. Come.

Come let me tell you what hoiy
Mr. *Herbert* faies of fuch dayes and
Flowers as thefe, and then we will
thank God that we enjoy them, and
walk to the River and fit down quietly and try to catch the other brace of
Trouts.

Sweet day, fo cool, fo calm, fo bright,
The bridal of the earth and skie,
Sweet dews fhal weep thy fall to night,
*   for thou muft die*

Sweet Rofe, whofe hew angry and brave
Bids the rafh gazer wipe his eye,
Thy root is ever in its grave,
*   and thou muft die.*

Sweet Spring, ful of fweet days & rofes,
A box where fweets compacted lie;
My Mufick fhewes you have your clofes,
*   and all muft die.*

Only a fweet and vertuous foul,
Like feafoned timber never gives,

I 4   *But*

But when the whole world turns to cole,
                          then chiefly lives.

Viat. I thank you, good Master,
for your good direction for fly-fishing, and for the sweet enjoyment of
the pleasant day, which is so far spent
without offence to God or man. and
I thank you for the sweet close of
your discourse with Mr. *Herberts*
Verses, which I have heard, loved
Angling; and I do the rather believe
it, because he had a spirit sutable to
Anglers, and to those Primitive
Christians that you love, and have
so much commended.

Pisc. Well, my loving Scholer,
and I am pleased to know that you
are so well pleased with my direction
and discourse; and I hope you
will be pleased too, if you find a
Trout at one of our Angles., which
we left in the water to fish for it self;
you shall chuse which shall be yours,
and it is an even lay, one catches;
                                    And

And let me tell you, this kind of fishing, and laying Night-hooks, are like putting money to ufe, for they both work for the Owners, when they do nothing but fleep, or eat, or rejoice, as you know we have done this laft hour, and fate as quietly and as free from cares under this *Sycamore*, as *Virgils Tityrus* and his *Melibæus* did under their broad *Beech* tree: No life, my honeft Scholer, no life fo happy and fo pleafant as the Anglers, unlefs it be the Beggers life in Summer; for then only they take no care, but are as happy as we Anglers.

Viat. Indeed Mafter, and fo they be, as is witneffed by the beggers Song, made long fince by *Frank Davifon*, a good Poet, who was not a Begger, though he were a good Poet.

Pifc. Can you fing it, Scholer?

Viat. Sit down a little, good Mafter, and I wii try.

Bright

Bright shines the Sun, play beggers, play,
here's scraps enough to serve to day:
What noise of viols is so sweet
As when our merry clappers ring?
What mirth doth want when beggers meet?
A beggers life is for a King:
Eat, drink and play, sleep when we list,
Go where we will so stocks be mist.
Bright shines the Sun, play beggers, &c

The world is ours and ours alone,
For we alone have world at will;
We purchase not, all is our own,
Both fields and streets we beggers fill:
Play beggers play, play beggers play,
here's scraps enough to serve to day.

A hundred herds of black and white
Upon our Gowns securely feed,
And yet if any dare us bite,
He dies therefore as sure as Creed:
Thus beggers Lord it as they please,
And only beggers live at ease:
Bright shines the Sun, play beggers play,
here's scraps enough to serve to day.

Pisc.

Pisc. I thank you good Scholer, this Song was well humor'd by the maker, and well remembred and sung by yuo; and I pray forget not the Ketch which you promised to make against night, for our Country man honest *Coridon* will expect your Ketch and my Song, which I must be forc'd to patch up, for it is so long since I learnt it, that I have forgot a part of it. But come, lets stretch our legs a little in a gentle walk to the River, and try what interest our Angles wil pay us for lending them so long to be used by the *Trouts.*

Viat. Oh me, look you Master, a fish, a fish.

Pisc. I marry Sir, that was a good fish indeed; if I had had the luck to have taken up that Rod, 'tis twenty to one he should not have broke my line by running to the Rods end, as you suffered him; I would have held him, unless he had been fellow

to

to the great *Trout* that is neer an ell long, which had his picture drawne, and now to be seen at mine Hoste *Rickabies* at the *George* in *Ware*; and it may be, by giving that *Trout* the Rod, that is, by casting it to him into the water, I might have caught him at the long run, for so I use alwaies to do when I meet with an over-grown fish, and you will learn to do so hereafter; for I tell you, Scholer, fishing is an Art, or at least, it is an Art to catch fish.

Viat. But, Master, will this *Trout* die, for it is like he has the hook in his belly?

Pisc. I wil tel you, Scholer, that unless the hook be fast in his very Gorge, he wil live, and a little time with the help of the water, wil rust the hook, & it wil in time wear away as the gravel does in the horse hoof, which only leaves a false quarter.

And now Scholer, lets go to my Rod. Look you Scholer, I have
a fish

a fifh too, but it proves a logger-
headed *Chub*; and this is not much
a mifs, for this wil pleafure fome
poor body, as we go to our lodging to meet our brother *Peter* and
honeft *Coridon*- Come, now bait
your hook again, and lay it into the
water, for it rains again, and we wil
ev'n retire to the *Sycamore* tree, and
there I wil give you more directions
concerning fifhing; for I would
fain make yon an Artift.

Viat. Yes, good Mafter, I pray
let it be fo.

CHAP.

CHAP. V.

Pifc. **VV**EL, Scholer, now we are fate downe and are at eafe, I fhall tel you a little more of *Trout* fifhing before I fpeak of the *Salmon* (which I purpofe fhall be next) and then of the *Pike* or *Luce.* You are to know, there is night as well as day-fifhing for a *Trout* , and that then the beft are out of their holds; and the manner of taking them is on the top of the water with a great *Lob* or *Garden worm*, or rather two; which you are to fifh for in a place where the water runs fomewhat quietly (for in a ftream it wil not be fo well difcerned.) I fay, in a quiet or dead place neer to fome fwift, there draw your bait over the top of the water to

and

and fro, and if there be a good *Trout* in the hole, he wil take it, especial-ly if the night be dark; for then he lies boldly neer the top of the water, watching the motion of any *Frog* or *Water-mouse*, or *Rat* betwixt him and the skie, which he hunts for if he sees the water but wrinkle or move in one of these dead holes, where the great *Trouts* usually lye neer to their hold.

And you must fish for him with a strong line, and not a little hook, and let him have time to gorge your hook, for he does not usually for-sake it, as he oft will in the day-fishing: and if the night be not dark, then fish so with an *Artificial fly* of a light colour; nay he will sometimes rise at a dead Mouse or a piece of cloth, or any thing that seemes to swim cross the water, or to be in mo-tion: this is a choice way, but I have not oft used it because it is void of the pleasures that such dayes as
these

thefe that we now injoy, afford an *Angler.*

And you are to know, that in *Hamp-fhire,* (which I think exceeds all *England* for pleafant Brooks, and ftore of *Trouts*) they ufe to catch *Trouts* in the night by the light of a Torch or ftraw, which when they have difcovered, they ftrike with a *Trout* fpear ; this kind of way they catch many, but I would not believe it till I was an eye-witnefs of it, nor like it now I have feen it.

Viat. But Mafter, do not *Trouts* fee us in the night?

Pifc. Yes, and hear, and fmel too, both then and in the day time, for *Gefner* obferves, the *Otter* fmels a fifh forty furlong off him in the water; and that it may be true, is affirmed by Sir *Francis Bacon* (in the eighth Century of his Natural Hiftory) who there proves, that waters may be the *Medium* of founds, by demonftrating it thus, *That if you knock*

two

two stones together very deep under the water, those that stand on a bank neer to that place may hear the noise without any diminution of it by the water. He also offers the like experiment concerning the letting an *Anchor* fall by a very long Cable or rope on a Rock, or the sand within the Sea: and this being so wel observed and demonstrated, as it is by that learned man, has made me to believe that Eeles unbed themselves, and stir at the noise of the Thunder, and not only as some think, by the motion or the stirring of the earth, which is occasioned by that Thunder.

And this reason of Sir *Francis Bacons* has made me crave pardon of *Exper.* 792 one that I laught at, for affirming that he knew *Carps* come to a certain place in a Pond to be fed at the ringing of a Bel; and it shall be a rule for me to make as little noise as I can when I am a fishing, until Sir *Francis Bacon* be confuted, which I

K shall

ſhal give any man leave to do,and ſo leave off this Philoſophical diſcourſe for a diſcourſe of fiſhing.

Of which my next ſhall be to tell you, it is certain, that certain fields neer *Lemſter*, a Town in *Hereford-ſhire*,are obſerved, that they make the Sheep that graze upon them more fat then the next, and alſo to bear finer Wool; that is to ſay, that that year in which they feed in ſuch a particular paſture, they ſhall yeeld finer wool then the yeer before they came to feed in it, and courſer again if they ſhall return to their former paſture, and again return to a finer wool being fed in the fine wool ground. Which I tell you,that you may the better believe that I am certain, If I catch a *Trout* in one Meadow, he ſhall be *white* and *faint*,and very like to be *lowſie*; and as certainly if I catch a *Trout* in the next Meadow, he ſhal be ſtrong,and *red*, and *luſty*, and much better meat: Truſt

Truſt me (Scholer) I have caught many a *Trout* in a particular Meadow, that the very ſhape and inamelled colour of him, has joyed me to look upon him, and I have with *Solomon* concluded , *Every thing is beautifull in his ſeaſon.*

It is now time to tell you next, (according to promiſe) ſome obſervations of the *Salmon* ; But firſt, I wil tel you there is a fiſh, called by ſome an *Umber*, and by ſome a *Greyling*, a choice fiſh, eſteemed by many to be equally good with the *Trout* : it is a fiſh that is uſually about eighteen inches long, he lives in ſuch ſtreams as the *Trout* does ; and is indeed taken with the ſame bait as a *Trout* is, for he will bite both at the *Minnow*, the *Worm*, and the *Fly*, both *Natural* and *Artificial* : of this fiſh there be many in *Trent*, and in the River that runs by *Salisbury*, and in ſome other leſ-

K 2 ſer

fer Brooks; but he is not fo general a fifh as the *Trout*, nor to me either fo good to eat, or fo pleafant to fifh for as the *Trout* is; of which two fifhes I will now take my leave, and come to my promifed Obfervations of the *Salmon*, and a little advice for the catching him.

CHAP.

CHAP. VI.

THE *Salmon* is ever bred in the fresh Rivers (and in most Rivers about the month of *August*) and never grows big but in the *Sea*; and there to an incredible bigness in a very short time; to which place they covet to swim, by the instinct of nature, about a set time: but if they be stopp'd by *Mills, Floud-gates* or *Weirs*, or be by accident lost in the fresh water, when the others go (which is usually by flocks or sholes) then they thrive not.

And the old *Salmon*, both the *Melter* and *Spawner*, strive also to get into the *Sea* before Winter; but being stopt that course, or lost; grov sick in fresh waters, and by degrees unseasonable, and kipper, that is, to have a bony griftle, to grow (not unlike a *Hauks* beak) on one of his chaps, which hinders him from feeding , and then he pines and dies.

But if he gets to *Sea*, then that griftle wears away, or is caft off (as the *Eagle* is faid to caft his bill) and he recovers his ftrength, and comes next Summer to the fame River, (if it be poffible) to enjoy the former pleafures that there poffeft him; for (as one has wittily obferved) he has (like fome perfons of Honour and Riches, which have both their winter and Summer houfes) the frefh Rivers for Summer, and the falt water for winter to fpend his life in; In his Hi-which is not (as Sir *Francis Bacon* ftory of hath obferved) above ten years: And Life and Death. it is to be obferved, that though they grow big in the *Sea*, yet they grow not fat but in frefh Rivers; and it is obferved, that the farther they get from the *Sea*, the better they be.

And

And it is obſerved, that, to the end they may get far from the *Sea*, either to Spawne or to poſſeſs the pleaſure that they then and there find, they will force themſelves over the tops of *Weirs*, or *Hedges*, or *ſtops* in the water, by taking their tails into their mouthes, and leaping over thoſe places, even to a height beyond common belief: and ſometimes by forcing themſelves againſt the ſtreame through Sluces and Floud-gates, beyond common credit. And 'tis obſerved by *Geſner*, that there is none bigger then in *England*, nor none better then in Thames.

And for the *Salmons* ſudden growth, it has been obſerved by tying a Ribon in the tail of ſome number of the young *Salmons*, which have becn taken in *Weires*, as they ſwimm'd towards the ſalt water, and then by taking a part of them again with the ſame mark, at the ſame

K 4   place

place, at their returne from the Sea, which is ufually about fix months after; and the like experiment hath been tried upon young *Swallows,* who have after fix months abfence, been oferved to return to the fame chimney, there to make their nefts, and their habitations for the Summer following; which hath inclined many to think, that every *Salmon* ufually returns to the fame River in which it was bred, as young *Pigeons* taken out of the fame *Dove-cote,* have alfo been obferved to do.

And you are yet to obferve further, that the He *Salmon* s ufually bigger then the Spawner, and that he is more kipper, & lefs able to endure a winter in the frefh water, then the She is; yet fhe is at that time of looking lefs kipper and better, as watry and as bad meat.

And yet you are to obferve, that as there is no general rule without an exception, fo there is fome few

Rivers

Rivers in this Nation that have *Trouts* and *Salmon* in feafon in winter. But for the obfervations of that and many other things, I muft in mannersomit,becaufetheywilprove too large for our narrow compafs of time, and therefore I fhall next fall upon my direction how to fifh for the *Salmon*.

And for that, firft, you fhall obferve, that ufually he ftaies not long in a place (as *Trouts* wil) but (as I faid) covets ftill to go neerer the Spring head; and that he does not (as the *Trout* and many other fifh) lie neer the water fide or bank, or roots of trees, but fwims ufually in the middle, and neer the ground; and that there you are to fifh for him ; and that he is to be caught as the *Trout* is, with a *Worm*, a *Minnow*, (which fome call a *Penke*) or with a *Fly*.

And you are to obferve, that he is very, very feldom obferved to bite

at

at a *Minnow* (yet fometime he will)
and not oft at a *fly*, but more ufually
at a *Worm*, and then moft ufually at
a *Lob* or *Garden worm*, which fhould
be wel fcowred, that is to fay, feven
or eight dayes in Mofs before you
fifh with them; and if you double
your time of eight into fixteen, or
more, into twenty or more days, it is
ftill the better, for the worms will ftil
be clearer, tougher, and more lively,
and continue fo longer upon your
hook.

And now I fhall tell you, that
which may be called a fecret: I have
been a fifhing with old *Oliver Henly*
(now with God) a noted Fifher,
both for *Trout* and *Salmon*, and have
obferved that he would ufually take
three or four worms out of his bag
and put them into a little box in his
pocket, where he would ufually let
them continue half an hour or more,
before he would bait his hook with
them; I have ask'd him his reafon,
and

and he has replied, *He did but pick the best out to be in a readiness against he baited his hook the next time* : But he has been obferved both by others, and my felf, to catch more fifh then I or any other body, that has ever gone a fifhing with him, could do, efpecially *Salmons*; and I have been told lately by one of his moft intimate and fecret friends, that the box in which he put thofe worms was anointed with a drop, or two, or three of the Oil of *Ivy-berries*, made by expreffion or infufion, and that by the wormes remaining in that box an hour, or a like time, they had incorporated a kind of fmel that was irrefiftibly attractive, enough to force any fifh, within the fmel of them, to bite. This I heard not long fince from a friend, but have not tryed it; yet I grant it probable, and refer my Reader to Sir *Francis Bacons* Natural Hiftory, where he proves fifhes may hear; and I am certain *Gefner* fayes

fayes, the *Otter* can fmell in the water, and know not that but fifh may do fo too : 'tis left for a lover of Angling, or any that defires to improve that Art, to try this conclufion.

I fhall alfo impart another experiment (but not tryed by my felfe) which I wil deliver in the fame words as it was by a friend, given me in writing.

Take the ftinking oil drawn out of Poly pody *of the Oak, by a retort mixt with* Turpentine, *and Hivehoney, and annoint your bait therewith, and it will doubtleffe draw the fifh to it.*

But in thefe things I have no great faith, yet grant it probable, and have had from fome chimical men (namely, from Sir *George Haftings* and others) an affirmation of them to be very advantageous: but no more of thefe, efpecially not in this place.

I might here, before I take my
leave

leave of the *Salmon*, tell you, that there is more then one fort of them, as namely, a *Tecon*, and another called in fome places a *Samlet*, or by fome, a *Skegger :* but thefe (and o-thers which I forbear to name) may be fifh of another kind, and differ, as we know a *Herring* and a *Pilcher* do; but muft by me be left to the difquifitions of men of more leifure and of greater abilities, then I pro-fefs my felf to have.

And laftly, I am to borrow fo much of your promifed patience, as to tell you, that the *Trout* or *Sal-mon*, being in feafon, have at their firft taking out of the water (which continues during life) their bodies adorned, the one with fuch red fpots, and the other with black or blackifh fpots, which gives them fuch an addition of natural beau-tie, as I (that yet am no enemy to it) think was never given to any woman by the Artificial Paint or
Patch-

Patches in which they ſo much pride themſelves in this age. And ſo I ſhall leave them and proceed to ſome Obſervations of the *Pike.*

CHAP. VII.

Piſc.　IT is not to be doubted but that the *Luce,* or *Pikrell,* or *Pike* breeds by Spawning; and yet *Geſner* ſayes, that ſome of them breed, where none ever was, out of a weed called *Pikrell-weed,* and other glutinous matter, which with the help of the Suns heat proves in ſome particular ponds (apted by nature for it) to become *Pikes.*

In his Hiſtory of Liſe and Death.　Sir *Francis Bacon* obſerves the *Pike* to be the longeſt lived of any freſh water fiſh, and yet that his life is not

not usually above fortie years; and yet *Gesner* mentions a *Pike* taken in *Swedeland* in the year 1449, with a Ring about his neck, declaring he was put into the Pond by *Frederick* the second, more then two hundred years before he was last taken, as the Inscription of that Ring, being Greek, was interpreted by the then Bishop of *Worms*. But of this no more, but that it is observed that the old or very great *Pikes* have in them more of state then goodness; the smaller or middle siz'd *Pikes* being by the most and choicest palates observed to be the best meat; but contrary, the Eele is observed to be the better for age and bigness.

All *Pikes* that live long prove chargeable to their keepers, because their life is maintained by the death of so many other fish, even those of his owne kind, which has made him by some Writers to bee called the *Tyrant* of the Rivers, or the *Fresh*

water

water-wolf, by reafon of his bold, greedy, devouring difpofition; which is fo keen, as *Gefner* relates, a man going to a Pond (where it feems a *Pike* had devoured all the fifh) to water his Mule, had a *Pike* bit his Mule by the lips, to which the *Pike* hung fo faft, that the *Mule* drew him out of the water, and by that accident the owner of the *Mule* got the *Pike*; I tell you who relates it, and fhall with it tel you what a wife man has obferved, *It is a hard thing to perfwade the belly, becaufe it hath no ears.*

But if this relation of *Gefners* bee dif-believed, it is too evident to bee doubted that a *Pike* will devoure a fifh of his own kind, that fhall be bigger then this belly or throat will receive; and fwallow a part of him, and let the other part remaine in his mouth till the fwallowed part be digefted, and then fwallow that other part that was in his mouth, and fo
put

put it over by degrees. And it is obferved, that the *Pike* will eat venemous things (as fome kind of *Frogs*
are) and yet live witnout being
harmed by them: for, as fome fay,
he has in him a natural Balfome or
Antidote againft all Poifon: and
others, that he never eats a venemous *Frog* till he hath firft killed
her, and then (as *Ducks* are obferved to do to *Frogs* in Spawning time,
at which time fome *Frogs* are obferved to be venemous) fo through-
ly wafht her, by tumbling her up and
down in the water, that he may devour her without danger. And
Gefner affirms, that a *Polonian* Gentleman did faithfully affure him, he
had feen two young Geefe at one
time in the belly of a *Pike*: and hee
obferves, that in *Spain* there is no
Pikes, and that the biggeft are in
the Lake *Thracimane* in *Italy*, and the
next, if not equal to them, are the
Pikes of *England*.

L   The

The *Pike* is alſo obſerved to be a melancholly, and a bold fiſh: Melancholly, becauſe he alwaies ſwims or reſts himſelfe alone, and never ſwims in ſholes, or with company, as *Roach*, and *Dace*, and moſt other fiſh do: And bold, becauſe he fears not a ſhadow, or to ſee or be ſeen of any body, as the *Trout* and *Chub*, and all other fiſh do.

And it is obſerved by *Geſner*, that the bones, and hearts, & gals of *Pikes* are very medicinable for ſeveral Diſeaſes, as to ſtop bloud, to abate Fevers, to cure Agues, to oppoſe or expel the infection of the Plague, and to be many wayes medicinable and uſeful for the good of mankind; but that the biting of a *Pike* is venemous and hard to be cured.

And it is obſerved, that the *Pike* is a fiſh that breeds but once a year, and that other fiſh (as namely *Loaches*) do breed oftner; as we are certaine Pigeons do almoſt every month, and yet

yet the Hawk, a bird of prey (as the *Pike* is of fish) breeds but once in twelve months: and you are to note, that his time of breeding or Spawning is usually about the end of *February*; or somewhat later, in *March*, as the weather proves colder or warmer: and to note, that his manner of breeding is thus, a He and a She *Pike* will usually go together out of a River into some ditch or creek, and that there the Spawner casts her eggs, and the Melter hovers over her all that time that she is casting her Spawn, but touches her not. I might say more of this, but it might be thought curiosity or worse, and shall therefore forbear it, and take up so much of your attention as to tell you that the best of *Pikes* are noted to be in Rivers, then those in great Ponds or Meres, and the worst in smal Ponds.

And now I shall proceed to

give

give you some directions how to
catch this *Pike*.

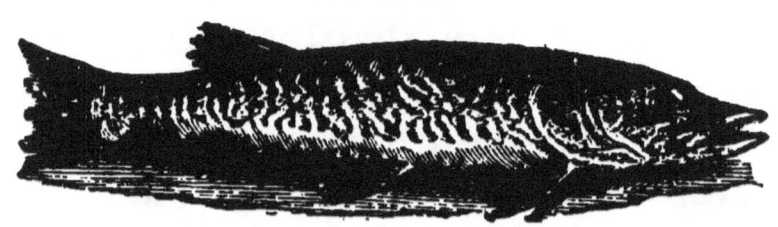

which you have with so much patience heard me talk of.

His feeding is usually *fish* or *frogs*,
and sometime a weed of his owne,
called *Pikrel-weed*, of which I told
you some think some *Pikes* are bred;
for they have observed, that where
no *Pikes* have been put into a Pond,
yet that there they have been found,
and that there has been plenty of
that

that weed in that Pond, and that that weed both breeds and feeds them; but whether thofe *Pikes* fo bred will ever breed by generation as the others do, I fhall leave to the difquifitions of men of more curio-fity and leifure then I profefs my felf to have; and fhall proceed to tell you, that you may fifh for a *Pike*, ei-ther with a ledger, or a walking-bait; and you are to note, that I call that a ledger which is fix'd, or made to reft in one certaine place when you fhall be abfent; and that I call that a walking bait, which you take with you, and have ever in motion. Con-cerning which two, I fhall give you this direction, That your ledger bait is beft to be a living bait, whe-ther it be a fifh or a Frog; and that you may make them live the longer, you may, or indeed you muft take this courfe:

Firft, for your live bait of fi h, a *Roch* or *Dace* is (I think) beft and moft

L 3 tempting,

tempting, and a *Pearch* the longeſt liv'd on a hook; you muſt take your knife, (which cannot be too ſharp) and betwixt the head and the fin on his back, cut or make an inſition,or ſuch a ſcar as you may put the arming wyer of your hook into it, with as little bruiſing or hurting the fiſh as Art and diligence will enable you to do, and ſo carrying your arming wyer along his back, unto, or neer the tail of your fiſh, betwixt the skin and the body of it, draw out that wyer or arming of your hook at another ſcar neer to his tail ; then tye him about it with thred,but no harder then of neceſſitie you muſt to prevent hurting the fiſh; and the better to avoid hurting the fiſh, ſome have a kind of probe to open the way, for the more eaſie entrance and paſſage of your wyer or arming: but as for theſe, time and a little experience will teach you better then I can by words ; for of this I will for the pre-

ſent

fent fay no more, but come next to
give you fome directions how to
bait your hook with a Frog.

Viat. But, good Mafter, did not
you fay even now, that fome *Frogs*
were venemous, and is it not dangerous to touch them?

Pifc. Yes, but I wil give you fome
Rules or Cautions concerning them :
And firft, you are to note, there is
two kinds of *Frogs* ; that is to fay,
(if I may fo exprefs my felf) a *flefh*
and a *fifh-frog*: by flefh *frogs*, I mean,
frogs that breed and live on the land ;
and of thefe there be feveral forts
and colours, fome being peckled,
fome greenifh, fome blackifh, or
brown : the green *Frog*, which is a
fmal one, is by *Topfell* taken to be
venemous ; and fo is the *Padock*, or
Frog-Padock, which ufually keeps
or breeds on the land, and is very
large and bony, and big, efpecially the She *frog* of that kind ; yet thefe
wil fometime come into the water,

L 4   but

but it is not often; and the land *frogs*
are some of them observed by him,
to breed by laying eggs, and others
to breed of the slime and dust of the
earth, and that in winter they turn
to slime again, and that the next
Summer that very slime returns to
be a living creature; this is the o-
pinion of *Pliny*: and* *Cardanus* undertakes to give reason for the raining of *Frogs*; but if it were in my
power, it should rain none but water
Frogs, for those I think are not venemous, especially the right water
Frog , which about *February* or
March breeds in ditches by slime and
blackish eggs in that slime, about
which time of breeding the He and
She *frog* are observed to use divers
simber salts, and to croke and make
a noise, which the land *frog*, or *Padock
frog* never does. Now of these water
Frogs, you are to chuse the yellowest
that you can get, for that the *Pike*
ever likes best. And thus use your
Frog,

In his 16th
Book, *De
subtil.ex.*

Frog, that he may continue long a-live :

Put your hook into his mouth, which you may eafily do from a-bout the middle of *April* till *Auguft,* and then the *Frogs* mouth grows up and he continues fo for at leaft fix months without eating, but is fu-ftained, none, but he whofe name is Wonderful, knows how. I fay, put yourhook, I mean the arming wire, through his mouth and out at his gills, and then with a fine needle and Silk fow the upper part of his leg with only one ftitch to the arm-ed wire of your hook, or tie the *frogs* leg above the upper joint to the armed wire, and in fo doing ufe him as though you loved him, that is, harme him as little as you may pof-fibly, that he may live the longer.

And now, having given you this direction for the baiting your ledger hook with a live fifh or frog, my next muft be to tell you, how your
hook

hook thus baited muſt or may be u-
ſed; and it is thus: Having faſtned
your hook to a line, which if it be not
fourteen yards long, ſhould not be
leſs then twelve; you are to faſten
that line to any bow neer to a hole
where a *Pike* is, or is likely to lye, or to
have a haunt, and then wind your line
on any forked ſtick, all yonr line, except a half yard of it, or rather more,
and ſplit that forked ſtick with ſuch a
nick or notch at one end of it, as may
keep the line from any more of it ra-
velling from about the ſtick, then ſo
much of it as you intended; and
chuſe your forked ſtick to be of that
bigneſs as may keep the *fiſh* or *frog*
from pulling the forked ſtick under
the water till the *Pike* bites, and
then the *Pike* having pulled the line
forth of the clift or nick in which it
was gently faſtened, will have line e-
nough to go to his hold and powch
the bait: and if you would have this
ledger bait to keep at a fixt place, un-
diſtur-

disturbed by wind or other acci-
dents, which may drive it to the
shoare side(for you are to note that
it is likeliest to catch a *Pike* in the
midst of the water) then hang a
small Plummet of lead, a stone, or
piece of tyle, or a turfe in a string,
and cast it into the water, with the
forked stick to hang upon the
ground, to be as an Anchor to keep
the forked stick from moving out of
your intended place till the *Pike*
come. This I take to be a very
good way, to use so many ledger
baits as you intend to make tryal of.

Or if you bait your hooks thus,
with live fish or Frogs, and in a
windy day fasten them thus to a
bow or bundle of straw, and by the
help of that wind can get them to
move crofs a *Pond* or *Mere,* you
are like to stand still on the shoar
and see sport, if there be any store of
Pikes; or these live baits may make
sport, being tied about the body or
wings

wings of a *Goose* or *Duck*, and she chafed over a Pond: and the like may be done with turning three or four live baits thus faftened to bladders, or boughs, or bottles of hay, or flags, to fwim down a *River*, whilft you walk quietly on the fhore along with them, and are ftill in expectation of fport. The reft muft be taught you by practice, for time will not alow me to fay more of this kind of fifhing with live baits.

And for your dead bait for a *Pike*, for that you may be taught by one dayes going a fifhing with me or any other body that fifhes for him, for the baiting your hook with a dead *Gudgion* or a *Roch*, and moving it up and down the water, is too eafie a thing to take up any time to direct you to do it; and yet, becaufe I cut you fhort in that, I will commute for it, by telling you that that was told me for a fecret: it is this:

Diffolve

Diſſolve Gum of Ivie *in Oyle of* Spike, *and therewith annoint your dead bait for a* Pike, *and then caſt it into a likely place, and when it has layen a ſhort time at the bottom, draw it towards the top of the water, and ſo up the ſtream, and it is more then likely that you have a* Pike *follow you with more then common eagerneſs.*

This has not been tryed by me, but told me by a friend of note, that pretended to do me a courteſie: but if this direction to catch a Pike thus do you no good, I am certaine this direction how to roſte him when he is caught, is choicely good, for I have tryed it, and it is ſomewhat the better for not being common ; but with my direction you muſt take this Caution, that your Pike muſt not be a ſmal one.

Firſt open your Pike *at the gills, and if need be, cut alſo a little ſlit towards his belly; out of theſe, take his guts, and keep his liver, which you*

are

are to shred very small with Time, Sweet Margerom, *and a little* Winter-Savoury; *to these put some pickled* Oysters, *and some* Anchovis, *both these last whole (for the* Anchovis *will melt, and the* Oysters *should not) to these you must add also a pound of sweet Butter, which you are to mix with the herbs that are shred, and let them all be well salted (if the* Pike *be more then a yard long, then you may put into these herbs more then a pound, or if he be less, then less Butter will suffice :) these being thus mixt, with a blade or two of* Mace, *must be put into the* Pikes *belly, and then his belly sowed up; then you are to thrust the spit through his mouth out at his tail; and then with four, or five, or six split sticks or very thin laths, and a convenient quantitie of tape or filiting, these laths are to be tyed round about the* Pikes *body, from his head to his tail, and the tape tied somewhat thick to prevent his breaking or failing off from the*

the spit; let him be rosted very leisurely, and often basted with Claret wine,
and Anchovis, and butter mixt together, and also with what moisture falls
from him into the pan : when you have
rosted him sufficiently, you are to hold
under him (when you unwind or cut
the tape that ties him) such a dish as
you purpose to eat him out of, and let
him fall into it with the sawce that is
rosted in his belly ; and by this means
the Pike will be kept unbroken and
complete ; then to the sawce, which
was within him, and also in the pan,
you are to add a fit quantity of the best
butter, and to squeeze the juice of three
or four Oranges : lastly, you may either put into the Pike with the Oysters, two cloves of Garlick, and take
it whole out when the Pike is cut off the
spit, or to give the sawce a hogoe, let
the dish (into which you let the Pike
fall) be rubed with it ; the using or
not using of this Garlick is left to your
discretion.

This

This diſh of meat is too good for any but Anglers or honeſt men; and, I truſt, you wil prove both, and therefore I have truſted you with this Secret. And now I ſhall proceed to give you ſome Obſervations concerning the *Carp*.

CHAP.

CHAP. VIII.

Pisc. THE *Carp* is a stately, a good, and a subtle fish, a fish that hath not (as it is said) been long in *England*, but said to be by one Mr. *Mascall* (a Gentleman then living at *Plumsted* in *Sussex*) brought into this Nation : and for the better confirmation of this, you are to remember I told you that *Gesner* sayes, there is not a *Pike* in *Spain*, and that except the Eele, which lives longest out of the water, there is none that will endure more hardness, or live longer then a *Carp* will out of it, and so the report of his being brought out of a forrain Nation into this, is the more probable.

Carps and *Loches* are observed to breed several months in one year,

M   which

which moft other fifh do not, and
it is the rather believed, becaufe
you fhall fcarce or never take a *Male
Carp* without a *Melt*, or a *Female*
without a *Roe* or *Spawn*; and for
the moft part very much, and efpecially all the Summer feafon; and
it is obferved, that they breed more
naturally in Ponds then in running
waters, and that thofe that live in
Rivers are taken by men of the
beft palates to be much the better
meat.

And it is obferved, that in fome
Ponds *Carps* will not breed, efpecially in cold Ponds; but where
they will breed, they breed innume-
rably, if there be no *Pikes* nor *Pearch*
to devour their Spawn, when it is
caft upon grafs, or flags, or weeds,
where it lies ten or twelve dayes before it be enlivened.

The *Carp*, if he have water room
and good feed, will grow to a very
great bignefs and length: I have
heard

heard, to above a yard long; though I never faw one above thirty three inches, which was a very great and goodly fifh.

Now as the increafe of *Carps* is wonderful for their number; fo there is not a reafon found out, I think, by any, why the fhould breed in fome Ponds, and not in others of the fame nature, for foil and all other circumftances; and as their breeding, fo are their decayes alfo very myfterious; I have both read it, and been told by a Gentleman of tryed honeftie, that he has knowne fixtie or more large *Carps* put into feveral Ponds neer to a houfe, where by reafon of the ftakes in the Ponds, and the Owners conftant being neer to them, it was impoffible they fhould be ftole away from him, and that when he has after three or four years emptied the Pond, and expected an increafe from them by breeding young ones (for that they might do so, he had, as the rule is, put in three Melters for one Spawner) he has, I say, after three or four years found neither a young nor old *Carp* remaining: And the like I have known of one that has almost watched his Pond, and at a like distance of time at the fishing of a Pond, found of seventy or eighty large *Carps*, not above five or six: and that he had forborn longer to fish the said Pond, but that he saw in a hot day in Summer, a large *Carp* swim neer to the top of the water with a *Frog* upon his head, and that he upon that occasion caused his Pond to be let dry: and I say, of seventie or eighty *Carps*, only found five or six in the said Pond, and those very sick and lean, and with every one a Frog sticking so fast on the head of the said *Carps*, that the Frog would not bee got off without extreme force or killing, and the Gentleman that did affirm this to me, told

me

me he faw it, and did declare his belief to be (and I alfo believe the
fame) that he thought the other
Carps that were fo ftrangely loft,
were fo killed by *Frogs* , and then
devoured.

But I am faln into this difcourfe
by accident, of which I might fay
more, but it has proved longer then
I intended, and poffibly may not to
you be confiderable; I fhall therefore give you three or four more
fhort obfervations of the *Carp,* and
then fall upon fome directions how
you hall fifh for him.

The age of *Carps* is by S. *Fran
cis Bacon* (in his Hiftory of Life and
Death)obferved to be but ten years;
yet others think they live longer:but
moft conclude, that(contrary to the
Pike or *Luce*) all *Carps* are the better for age and bignefs; the tongues
of *Carps* are noted to be choice and
coftly meat, efpecially to them that
buy them; but *Gefner* fayes, *Carps*

M 3   have

have no tongues like other fith, but a piece of flefh-like-fifh in their mouth like to a tongue, and may be fo called, but it is certain it is choicely good, and that the *Carp* is to be reckoned amongft thofe leather mouthed fifh, which I told you have their teeth in their throat, and for that reafon he is very feldome loft by breaking his hold, if your hook bee once ftuck into his chaps.

I told you, that Sir *Francis Bacon* thinks that the *Carp* lives but ten years; but *Janus Dubravius* (a *Germane* as I think) has writ a book in Latine of Fifh and Fifh Ponds, in which he fayes, that *Carps* begin to Spawn at the age of three yeers, and continue to do fo till thirty; he fayes alfo, that in the time of their breeding, which is in Summer when the Sun hath warmed both the earth and water, and fo apted them alfo for generation, that then three or

four

four Male *Carps* will follow a Female,
and that then fhe putting on a feem-
ing coynefs, they force her through
weeds and flags, where fhe lets fall
her eggs or Spawn, which fticks faft
to the weeds, and then they let fall
their Melt upon it, and fo it be-
comes in a fhort time to be a living
fifh ; and, as I told you, it is
thought the *Carp* does this feveral
months in the yeer, and moft believe that moft fifh breed after this
manner, except the Eele: and it is
thought that all *Carps* are not bred
by generation , but that fome
breed otherwayes, as fome *Pikes*
do.

Much more might be faid out of
him, and out of *Ariftotle*, which
Dubravius often quotes in his Difcourfe, but it might rather perplex
then fatisfie you, and therefore I
fhall rather chufe to direct you how
to catch , then fpend more time in

M 4   dif-

difcourfing either of the nature or the breeding of this *Carp,*

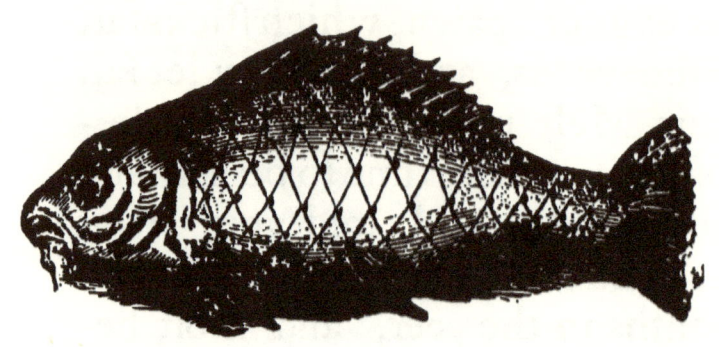

or of any more circumftances concerning him, but yet I fhall remember you of what I told you before, that he is a very fubtle fifh and hard to be caught.

And my firft direction is, that if you will fifh for a *Carp,* you muft put on a very large meafure of *patience,* efpecially to fifh for a *River Carp:* I have knowne a very good Fifher angle

angle diligently four or six hours in
a day, for three or four dayes together for a *River Carp*, and not have a
bite: and you are to note, that in
some Ponds it is as hard to catch a
Carp as in a River; that is to say,
where they have store of feed, & the
water is of a clayish colour; but you
are to remember, that I have told you
there is no rule without an exception,
and therefore being possest with that
hope and patience which I wish to
all Fishers, especially to the *Carp-
Angler*, I shall tell you with what
bait to fish for him; but that must
be either early or ate, and let me
tell you, that in hot weather (for he
will seldome bite in cold) you cannot bee too early or too late at
it.

The *Carp* bites either at wormes
or at Paste; and of worms I think
the blewish Marsh or Meadow worm
is best; but possibly another worm
not too big may do as well, and so
may

may a Gentle: and as for Paftes,
there are almoft as many forts as
there are Medicines for the Tooth-
ach, but doubtlefs fweet Paftes are
beft; I mean, Paftes mixt with honey, or with Sugar; which, that
you may the better beguile this
crafty fifh, fhould be thrown into the
Pond or place in which you fifh for
him fome hours before you under-
take your tryal of skil by the Angle-
Rod: and doubtlefs, if it be thrown
into the water a day or two before, at
feveral times, and in fmal pellets,
you are the likelier when you fifh
for the *Carp*, to obtain your defired
fport: or in a large Pond, to draw
them to any certain place, that they
may the better and with more hope
be fifhed for: you are to throw into
it, in fome certaine place, either
grains, or bloud mixt with Cow-
dung, or with bran; or any Garbage,
as Chickens guts or the like, and
then fome of your fmal fweet pellets,
with

with which you purpofe to angle;
thefe fmal pellets, being few of them
thrown in as you are Angling.

And your Paʃte muʃt bee thus
made : Take the fleʃh of a Rabet
or Cat cut fmal, and Bean-flower, or
(if not eafily got then) other flowre,
and then mix thefe together, and put
to them either Sugar, or Honey,
which I think better, and then beat
thefe together in a Mortar; or fometimes work them in your hands,
(your hands being very clean) and
then make it into a ball, or two, or
three, as you like beʃt for your ufe:
but you muʃt work or pound it fo
long in the Mortar, as to make it fo
tough as to hang upon your hook
without waʃhing from it, yet not too
hard; or that you may the better
keep it on your hook , you may
kneade with your Paʃte a little (and
not much) white or yellowiʃh wool.

And if you would have this Paʃte
keep all the year for any other fiʃh ,
then

then mix with it *Virgins-wax* and *clarified honey*, and work them together with your hands before the fire; then make thefe into balls, and it will keep all the yeer.

And if you fifh for a *Carp* with Gentles, then put upon your hook a fmall piece of Scarlet about this bignefs ▮ , it being foked in, or annointed with *Oyl of Peter*, called by some, *Oyl of the Rock*; and if your Gentles be put two or three dayes before into a box or horn anointed with Honey, and fo put upon your hook, as to preferve them to be living , you are as like to kill this craftie fifh this way as any other; but ftill as you are fifhing, chaw a little white or brown bread in your mouth, and caft it into the Pond about the place where your flote fwims. Other baits there be, but thefe with diligence , and patient watchfulnefs, will do it as well as any as I have ever practifed , or

heard

heard of: and yet I fhall tell you, that the crumbs of white bread and honey made into a Pafte, is a good bait for a *Carp,* and you know it is more eafily made. And having faid thus much of the *Carp,* my next difcourfe fhal be of the *Bream,* which fhall not prove fo tedious, and therefore I defire the continuance of your attention.

CHAP.

CHAP. IX.

Pifc. THE *Bream* being at a full growth , is a large and ftately fifh, he will breed both in Rivers and Ponds , but loves beft to live in Ponds, where, if he likes the aire, he will grow not only to be very large, but as fat as a Hog : he is by *Gefner* taken to be more pleafant or fweet then wholefome; this fifh is long in growing , but breeds exceedingly in a water that pleafes him, yea, in many Ponds fo faft, as to over ftore them, and ftarve the other fifh.

The Baits good for to catch the *Bream* are many ; as namely, young Wafps, and a Pafte made of brown bread and honey, or Gentels, or
efpecially

especially a worm, a worm that is not much unlike a Magot, which you will find at the roots of *Docks*, or of *Flags*, or of *Rushes* that grow in the water, or watry places, and a *Grashopper* having his legs nip'd off, or a flye that is in *June* and *July* to be found amongst the green Reed, growing by the water side, those are said to bee excellent baits. I doubt not but there be many others that both the *Bream* and the *Carp* also would bite at; but these time and expe rience will teach you how to find out : And so having according to my promise given you these short Observations concerning the *Bream*, I shall also give you some Observations concerning the *Tench*, and those also very briefly.

The *Tench* is observed to love to live in Ponds; but if he be in a River, then in the still places of the River, he is observed to be a Physician to other

other fifhes, and is fo called by many that have been fearchers into the nature of fifh; and it is faid, that a *Pike* will neither devour nor hurt him, becaufe the *Pike* being fick or hurt by any accident, is cured by touching the *Tench,* and the *Tench* does the like to other fifhes, either by touching them, or by being in their company.

Randelitius fayes in his difcourfe of fifhes (quoted by *Gefner*) that at his being at *Rome,* he faw certaine Jewes apply *Tenches* to the feet of a fick man for a cure; and it is obferved, that many of thofe people have many Secrets unknown to Chriftians, fecrets which have never been written, but have been fuccefsfively fince the dayes of *Solomon* (who knew the nature of all things from the Shrub to the Cedar) delivered by tradition from the father to the fon, and fo from generation to generation without writing, or (unlefs

it

it were cafually) without the leaſt
communicating them to any other
Nation or Tribe (for to do fo, they
account a profanation) *:* yet this
fiſh, that does by a natural inbred
Balſome, not only cure himſelfe if
he be wounded, but others alſo,
loves not to live in clear ſtreams pa-
ved with gravel, but in ſtanding waters, where mud and the worſt of
weeds abound, and therefore it is, I
think, that this *Tench*

is by fo many accounted better for
N   Medi-

Medicines then for meat: but for the firſt, I am able to ſay little; and for the later, can ſay poſitively, that he eats pleaſantly; and will therefore give you a few, and but a few directions how to catch him.

He will bite at a Paſte made of brown bread and honey, or at a Marſh-worm, or a Lob-worm; he will bite alſo at a ſmaller worm, with his head nip'd off, and a Cod-worm put on the hook before the worm; and I doubt not but that he will alſo in the three hot months (for in the nine colder he ſtirs not much) bite at a Flag-worm, or at a green Gentle, but can poſitively ſay no more of the *Tench*, he being a fiſh that I have not often Angled for; but I wiſh my honeſt Scholer may, and be ever fortunate when hee fiſhes.

Viat. I thank you good Maſter: but I pray Sir, ſince you ſee it ſtill rains *May* butter, give me ſome ob-

ſervafervations and directions concerning the *Pearch*, for they fay he is both a very good and a bold biting fifh, and I would faine learne to fifh for him.

Pifc. You fay true, Scholer, the *Pearch* is a very good, and a very bold biting fifh, he is one of the fifhes of prey, that, like the *Pike* and *Trout*, carries his teeth in his mouth, not in his throat, and dare venture to kill and devour another fifh; this fifh, and the *Pike* are (fayes *Gefner*) the beft of frefh water fifh; he Spawns but once a year, and is by Phyficians held very nutritive; yet by many to be hard of digeftion: They abound more in the River *Poe*, and in *England*, (fayes *Randelitius*) then other parts, and have in their brain a ftone, which is in forrain parts fold by Apothecaries, being there noted to be very medicinable againft the ftone in the reins: Thefe be a part of the commendati-

N 2   ons

ons which fome Philofophycal brain have beftowed upon the frefh-water *Pearch*, yet they commend the Sea *Pearch*, which is known by having but one fin on his back, (of which they fay, we *Englifh* fee but a few) to be a much better fifh.

The *Pearch* grows flowly, yet will grow, as I have been credibly informed, to be almoft two foot long; for my Informer told me, fuch a one was not long fince taken by Sir *Abraham Williams*, a Gentleman of worth, and a lover of Angling, that yet lives, and I wifh he may: this was a deep bodied fifh; and doubtlefs durft have devoured a *Pike* of half his own length ; for I have told you, he is a bold fifh, fuch a one, as but for extreme hunger, the *Pike* will not devour; for to affright the *Pike*, the *Pearch* will fet up his fins, much like as a *Turkie-Cock* wil fometimes fet up his tail.

But , my Scholer, the *Pearch* is not

not only valiant to defend himself,
but he is (as you said) a bold biting
fish, yet he he will not bite at all sea-
sons of the yeer; he is very abstemi-
ous in Winter; and hath been observed by some, not usually to bite
till the *Mulberry tree* buds, that is to
say, till extreme Frosts be past for
that Spring; for when the *Mulberry
tree* blossomes, many Gardners observe their forward fruit to be past the
danger of Frosts, and some have
made the like observation of the
Pearches biting.

But bite the *Pearch* will, and that
very boldly, and as one has wittily
observed, if there be twentie or fortie in a hole, they may be at one
standing all catch'd one after another; they being, as he saies, like the
wicked of the world, not afraid,
though their fellowes and compa-
nions perish in their sigh

N 3   And

And the baits for this bold fifh

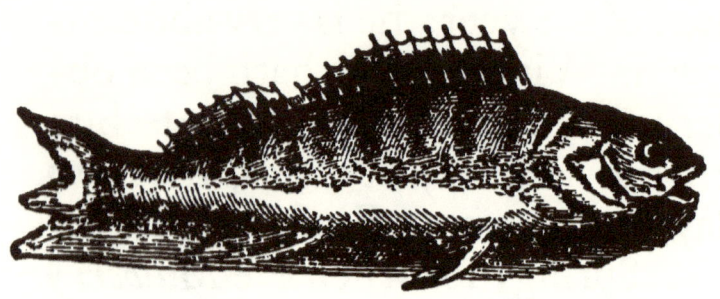

arc not many; I mean, he will bite as well at fome, or at any of thefe three, as at any or all others what-foever; a *Worm*, a *Minnow*, or a little *Frog* (of which you may find many in hay time) and of *worms*, the Dunghill worm, called a *brandling*, I take to be beft, being well fcow-red in Mofs or Fennel; and if you fifh for a *Pearch* with a *Minnow*, then it is beft to be alive. you fticking
your

your hook through his back fin, and letting him fwim up and down about mid-water, or a little lower, and you ftill keeping him to about that depth, by a Cork, which ought not to be a very light one: and the like way you are to fifh for the *Pearch* with a fmall *Frog*, your hook being faftened through the skin of his leg, towards the upper part of it: And laftly, I will give you but this advife, that you give the *Pearch* time enough when he bites, for there was fcarfe ever a-ny *Angler* that has given him too much. And now I think beft to reft my felfe, for I have almoft fpent my fpirits with talking fo long.

Viat. Nay, good Mafter, one fifh more, for you fee it rains ftill, and you know our Angles are like money put to ufury; they may thrive though we fit ftill and do no-thing, but talk & enjoy one another.

N 4   Come,

Come, come the other fifh, good
Mafter.

Pifc. But Scholer, have you
nothing to mix with this Difcourfe,
which now grows both tedious and
tirefome ? fhall I have nothing
from you that feems to have both
a good memorie, and a chearful
Spirit?

Viat. Yes, Mafter, I will fpeak
you a Coppie of Verfes that
were made by Doctor *Donne,* and
made to fhew the world that hee
could make foft and fmooth Verfes,
when he thought them fit and worth
his labour; and I love them the better, becaufe they allude to Rivers,
and fifh, and fifhing. They bee
thefe :

Come live with me; and be my love,
And we will fome new pleafures prove,
Of golden fands, and Chriftal brooks,
With filken lines and filver hooks.

There

There will the River wispering run,
Warm'd by thy eyes more then the Sun;
And there th' inamel'd fish wil stay,
Begging themselves they may betray.

When thou wilt swim in that live bath,
Each fish, which every channel hath
Most amorously to thee will swim,
Gladder to catch thee, then thou him.

If thou, to be so seen, beest loath
By Sun or Moon, thou darknest both;
And, if mine eyes have leave to see,
I need not their light, having thee.

Let others freeze with Angling Reeds,
And cut their legs with shels & weeds,
Or treacherously poor fish beset,
With strangling snares, or windowy net.

Let coarse bold hands, from slimy nest,
The bedded fish in banks outwrest,
Let curious Traitors sleave silk flies,
To 'witch poor wandring fishes eyes.

For

For thee, thou needſt no ſuch deceit,
For thou thy ſelf art thine own bait ;
Tha fiſh that is not catch'd thereby,
Is wiſer far, alas, then I.

Piſc. Well remem:bred, honeſt Scholer, I thank you for theſe choice Verſes, which I have heard formerly, but had quite forgot, till they were recovered by your happie memorie. Well, being I have now reſted my ſelf a little, I will make you ſome requital, by telling you ſome obſervations of the *Eele,* for it rains ſtill, and (as you ſay) our Angles are as money put to Uſe, that thrive when we play.

CHAP.

C H A P. X.

IT is agreed by moſt men, that the *Eele* is both a good and a moſt daintie fiſh; but moſt men differ about his breeding; ſome ſay, they breed by generation as other fiſh do; and others, that they breed (as ſome worms do) out of the putrifaction of the earth, and divers other waies; thoſe that denie them to breed by generation, as other fiſh do, ask, if any man ever ſaw an *Eel* to have Spawn or Melt? and they are anſwered, That they may be as certain of their breeding, as if they had ſeen Spawn; for they ſay, that they are certain that *Eeles* have all parts fit for generation , like other fiſh, but ſo ſmal as not to be eaſily diſcerned, by reaſon of their fatneſs; but that diſcerned they may

be

be; and that the Hee and the She *Eele* may be diftinguifhed by their fins.

And others fay, that *Eeles* growing old, breed other *Eeles* out of the corruption of their own age, which Sir *Francis Bacon* fayes, exceeds not ten years. And others fay, that *Eeles* are bred of a particular dew falling in the Months of *May* or *June* on the banks of fome particular Ponds or Rivers (apted by nature for that end) which in a few dayes is by the Suns heat turned into *Eeles*. I have feen in the beginning of *July*, in a River not far from *Canterbury*, fome parts of it covered over with young *Eeles* about the thicknefs of a ftraw; and thefe *Eeles* did lye on the top of that water, as thick as motes are faid to be in the Sun; and I have heard the like of other Rivers, as namely, in *Severn*, and in a *pond* or *Mere* in *Stafford-fhire*, where about a fet time in Summer, fuch fmall

Eeles

Eeles abound fo much, that many of the poorer fort of people, that inhabit near to it, take fuch *Eeles* out of this Mere, with fieves or fheets, and make a kind of *Eele-cake* of them, and eat it like as bread. And *Gefner* quotes venerable *Bede* to fay, that in *England* there is an Iland called *Ely*, by reafon of the innumerable number of *Eeles* that breed in it. But that *Eeles* may be bred as fome worms and fome kind of *Bees* and *Wafps* are, either of dew, or out of the corruption of the earth, feems to be made probable by the *Barnacles* and young *Goflings* bred by the Suns heat and the rotten planks of an old Ship, and hatched of trees, both which are related for truths by *Dubartas*, and our learned *Cambden*, and laborious *Gerrard* in his *Herball*.

It is faid by *Randelitius*, that thofe *Eeles* that are bred in Rivers, that relate to, or be neer to the Sea, never

ver return to the freſh waters (as the *Salmon* does alwaies deſire to do) when they have once taſted the ſalt water; and I do the more eaſily believe this, becauſe I am certain that powdered Bief is a moſt excellent bait to catch an *Eele* : and Sʳ. *Francis Bacon* will allow the *Eeles* life to be but ten years; yet he in his Hiſtory of Life and Death, mentions a *Lamprey*, belonging to the *Roman* Emperor, to be made tame, and ſo kept for almoſt three ſcore yeers; and that ſuch uſeful and pleaſant obſervations were made of this *Lamprey*, that *Craſſus* the Oratour (who kept her) lamented her death.

It is granted by all, or moſt men, that *Eeles*, for about ſix months (that is to ſay, the ſix cold months of the yeer) ſtir not up and down, neither in the Rivers nor the Pools in which they are, but get into the ſoft earth or mud, and there many of them together bed themſelves, and live with-

without feeding upon any thing (as I have told you some *Swallows* have been observed to do in hollow trees for those six cold months); and this the *Eele* and *Swallow* do, as not being able to endure winter weather; for *Gesner* quotes *Albertus* to say, that in the yeer 1125 (that years winter being more cold then usual) *Eeles* did by natures instinct get out of the water into a stack of hay in a Meadow upon dry ground, and there bedded themselves, but yet at last died there. I shall say no more of the *Eele*, but that, as it is observed, he is impatient of cold, so it has been observed, that in warm weather an *Eele* has been known to live five days out of the water. And lastly, let me tell you, that some curious searchers into the natures of fish, observe that there be several sorts or kinds of *Eeles*, as the *silver-Eele*, and green or *greenish Eel* (with which the River of Thames abounds, and

are

are called *Gregs*); and a blackifh *Eele*, whofe head is more flat and bigger then ordinary *Eeles*; and alfo an *Eele* whofe fins are redifh, and but feldome taken in this Nation (and yet taken fometimes): Thefe feveral kinds of *Eeles*, are (fay fome) diverfly bred; as namely, out of the corruption of the earth, and by dew, and other wayes ⸤as I have faid to you:⸥ and yet it is affirmed by fome, that for a certain, the *Silver-Eele* breeds by generation, but not by Spawning as other fifh do, but that her Brood come alive from her no bigger nor longer then a pin, and I have had too many teftimonies of this to doubt the truth of it.

And this *Eele* of which I have faid fo much to you, may be caught with divers kinds of baits; as namely, with powdered Bief, with a *Lob* or *Garden-worm*, with a *Minnow*, or gut of a *Hen*, *Chicken*, or with almoft

any

any thing, for he is a greedy fifh: but the *Eele* feldome ftirs in the day, but then hides himfelfe, and therefore he is ufually caught by night, with one of thefe baits of which I have fpoken, and then caught by laying hooks, which you are to faften to the bank, or twigs of a tree; or by throwing a ftring crofs the ftream, with many hooks at it, and baited with the forefaid baits, and a clod or plummet, or ftone, thrown into the River with this line, that fo you may in the morning find it neer to fome fixt place, and then take it up with a drag-hook or otherwife: but thefe things are indeed too common to be fpoken of; and an hours fifhing with any *Angler* will teach you better, both for thefe, and many other common things in the practical part of *Angling*, then a weeks difcourfe. I fhall therefore conclude this direction for taking the *Eele*, by telling you, that in a warm

O day

day in Summer, I have taken many a good *Eele* by *fnigling*, and have been much pleafed with that fport.

And becaufe you that are but a young Angler, know not what *fnigling* is, I wil now teach it to you: you remember I told you that *Eeles* do not ufually ftir in the day time, for then they hide themfelvs under fome covert, or under boards, or planks about Floud-gates, or Weirs, or Mils, or in holes in the River banks; and you obferving your time in a warm day, when the water is loweft, may take a hook tied to a ftrong line, or to a ftring about a yard long, and then into one of thefe holes, or between any boards about a Mill, or under any great ftone or plank, or any place where you think an *E le* may hide or fhelter her felfe, there with the help of a fhort ftick put in your bait, but leifurely, and as far as vou may conveniently; and it is

scarce

ſcarce to be doubted, but that if there be an *Fel* within the ſight of it, the *Eele* will bite inſtantly, and as certainly gorge it; and you need not doubt to have him, if you pull him not out of the hole too quickly, but pull him out by degrees, for he ly-ing folded double in his hole, will, with the help of his taile, break all, unleſs you give him time to be wea-ried with pulling, and ſo get him out by degrees; not pulling too hard. And thus much for this preſent time concerning the *Eele*: I wil next tel you a little of the *Barbell*, and hope with a little diſcourſe of him, to have an end of this ſhowr, and fal to fiſh-ing, for the weather clears up a little.

O 2　　CHAP.

CHAP. XI.

Pisc. THE *Barbell,* is so called (sayes *Gesner*) from
or by reason of his
beard, or wattles at his mouth, his
mouth being under his nose or chaps,
and he is one of the leather mouthed
fish that has his teeth in his throat, he
loves to live in very swift streams,
and where it is gravelly, and in the
gravel will root or dig with his nose
like a Hog, and there nest himself,
taking so fast hold of any weeds or
moss that grows on stones, or on
piles about *Weirs,* or *Floud-gates,* or
Bridges, that the water is not able, be
it never so swift, to force him from
the place which he seems to contend
for : this is his constant custome in
Summer, when both he, and most
living creatures joy and sport themselves

felves in the Sun ; but at the approach of Winter, then he forfakes the fwift ftreams and fhallow waters, and by degrees retires to thofe parts of the River that are quiet and deeper; in which places, (and I think about that time) he Spawns ; and as I have formerly told you, with the help of the Melter, hides his Spawn or eggs in holes, which they both dig in the gravel, and then they mutually labour to cover it with the fame fand to prevent it from being devoured by other fifh.

There be fuch ftoie of this fifh in the River *Danubie*, that *Randelitius* fayes, they may in fome places of it, and in fome months of the yeer, be taken by thofe that dwel neer to the River, with their hands, eight or ten load at a time; he fayes, they begin to be good in *May*, and that they ceafe to be fo in *Auguft* ; but it is found to be otherwife in this Nation: but thus far we agree with him, that the

Spawn

Spawne of a *Barbell* is, if he not poifon, as he fayes, yet that it is dangerous meat, and efpecially in the month of *May*; and *Gefner* declares, it had an ill effect upon him, to the indangering of his life.

This fifh is of a fine caft and handfome fhape,

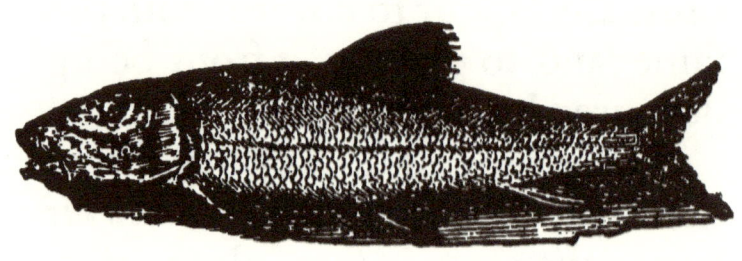

and may be rather faid not to be ill, then to bee good meat; the *Chub* and he have (I think) both loft a part of their credit by ill Cookery, they

they being reputed the worſt or
coarſeſt of freſh water fiſh : but the
Barbell affords an *Angler* choice
ſport, being a luſtie and a cunning
fiſh ; ſo luſtie and cunning as to en-
danger the breaking of the Anglers
line, by running his head forcibly
towards any covert or hole, or bank,
and then ſtriking at the line, to break
it off with his tail (as is obſerved by
Plutark, in his book *De induſtria a-
nimalium*) and alſo ſo cunning to
nibble and ſuck off your worme
cloſe to the hook, and yet avoid
the letting the huck come into his
mouth.

The *Barbell* is alſo curious for his
baits, that is to ſay, that they be
clean and ſweet; that is to ſay, to
have your worms well ſcowred, and
not kept in ſowre or muſtie moſs ;
for at a well ſcowred Lob-worm, he
will bite as boldly as at any bait, e-
ſpecially, if the night or two before
you fiſh for him, you ſhall bait the

O 4   places

places where you intend to fifh for
him with big worms cut into pieces;
and Gentles (not being too much
fcowred, but green) are a choice bait
for him, and fo is cheefe, which is
not to be too hard, but kept a day
or two in a wet linnen cloth to make
it tough; with this you may alfo
bait the water a day or two before
you fifh for the *Barbel*, and be much
the likelier to catch ftore; and if the
cheefe were laid in clarified honey
a fhort time before (as namely, an
hour or two) you were ftill the likelier to catch fifh; fome have directed to cut the cheefe into thin pieces, and tofte it, and then tye it on
the hook with fine Silk: and fome
advife to fifh for the *Barbell* with
Sheeps tallow and foft cheefe beaten
or work'd into a Pafte, and that it
is choicely good in *Auguft*; and I.
believe it: but doubtlefs the Lob-
worm well fcoured, and the Gentle
not too much fcowred, and cheefe
ordered

ordered as I have directed, are baits
enough, and I think will ferve in a-
ny Month; though I fhall commend
any Angler that tryes conclufions,
and is induftrious to improve the
Art. And now, my honeft Scholer,
the long fhowre, and my tedious
difcourfe are both ended together ;
and I fhall give you but this Obfervation, That when you fifh for a
Barbell, your Rod and Line be both
long, and of good ftrength, for you
will find him a heavy and a doged
fifh to be dealt withal, yet he feldom
or never breaks his hold if he be once
ftrucken.

And now lets go and fee what in-
tereft the *Trouts* will pay us for letting our *Angle-rods* lye fo long and
fo quietly in the water. Come ,
Scholer; which will you take up ?

Viat. Which you think fit, Mafter.

Pifc. Why, you fhall take up
that ; for I am certain by viewing
the

the Line, it has a fish at it. Look you, Scholer, well done. Come now, take up the other too; well, now you may tell my brother *Peter* at night, that you have caught a leafe of *Trouts* this day. And now lets move toward our lodging, and drink a draught of *Red-Cows milk*, as we go, and give pretty *Maudlin* and her mother a brace of *Trouts* for their fupper.

Viat. Mafter, I like your motion very well, and I think it is now about milking time, and yonder they be at it.

Pifc. God fpeed you good woman, I thank you both for our Songs laft night; I and my companion had fuch fortune a fifhing this day, that we refolve to give you and *Maudlin* a brace of *Trouts* for fupper, and we will now tafte a draught of your *Red Cows milk.*

Milkw. Marry, and that you fhal with all my heart, and I will be ftill

your

your debtor: when you come next this way, if you will but fpeak the word, I will make you a good *Silla-bub*, and then you may fit down in a *Hay-cock* and eat it, and *Maudlin* fhal fit by and fing you the good old Song of the *Hunting in Chevy Chafe*, or fome other good Ballad, for fhe hath good ftore of them: *Maud-lin* hath a notable memory.

Viat. We thank you, and intend once in a Month to call upon you again, and give you a little warning, and fo good night; good night *Maudlin.* And now, good Mafter, lets lofe no time, but tell me fome-what more of fifhing; and if you pleafe, firft fomething of fifhing for a *Gudgion.*

Pifc. I will, honeft Scholer. The *Gudgion* is an excellent fifh to eat, and good alfo to enter a young *Angler*; he is eafie to bee taken with a fmal red worm at the ground and is one of thofe leather mouthed fifh

fifh that has his teeth in his throat and will hardly be loft off from the hook if he be once ftrucken: they be ufually fcattered up and down every River in the fhallows, in the heat of Summer; but in *Autome*, when the weeds begin to grow fowre or rot, and the weather colder, then they gather together, and get into the deeper parts of the water, and are to be fifh'd for there, with your hook alwaies touching the ground, if you fifh for him with a flote or with a cork; but many will fifh for the *Gudgion* by hand, with a running line upon the ground without a cork as a *Trout* is fifhed for, and it is an excellent way.

There is alfo another fifh called a *Pope*, and by fome a *Ruffe*, a fifh that is not known to be in fome Rivers; it is much like the *Pearch* for his fhape, but will not grow to be bigger then a *Gudgion*; he is an excellent fifh, no fifh that fwims is of a
pleafanter

pleafanter tafte; and he is alfo
excellent to enter a young *Angler*,
for he is a greedy biter, and they
will ufually lye abundance of them
together in one referved place where
the water is deep, and runs quietly,
and an eafie Angler, if he has found
where they lye, may catch fortie or
fiftie, or fometimes twice fo many at
a ftanding.

There is alfo a *Bleak*, a fifh that is
ever in motion, and therefore called by fome the River Swallow; for
juft as you fhall obferve the *Swallow*
to be moft evenings in Summer ever
in motion, making fhort and quick
turns when he flies to catch flies in
the aire, by which he lives, fo does
the *Bleak* at the top of the water;
and this fifh is beft caught with a
fine fmal Artificial Fly, which is to
be of a brown colour, and very
fmal, and the hook anfwerable:
There is no better fport then whip-
ping for *Bleaks* in a boat in a Sum-
ners

mers evening, with a hazle top about five or fix foot long, and a line twice the length of the Rod. I have heard Sir *Henry Wotton* fay, that there be many that in *Italy* will catch *Swallows* fo, or efpecially *Martins* (the Bird-Angler ftanding on the top of a Steeple to do it, and with a line twice fo long, as I have fpoke of) and let me tell you, Scholer, that both *Martins* and *Blekes* be moft excellent meat.

I might now tell you how to catch *Roch* and *Dace*, and fome other fifh of little note, that I have not yet fpoke of; but you fee we are almoft at our lodging, and indeed if we were not, I would omit to give you any directions concerning them, or how to fiih for them, not but that they be both good fifh (being in feafon) and efpecially to fome palates, and they alfo make the Angler good fport (and you know the Hunter fayes, there is more fport in hunting

the

the Hare, then in eating of her) but I will forbear to give you any directi-on concerning them, becaufe you may go a few dayes and take the pleafure of the frefh aire, and bear any common Angler company that fifhes for them, and by that means learn more then any direction I can give you in words, can make you capable of; and I will there-fore end my difcourfe, for yonder comes our brother *Peter* and honeft *Coridon*, but I will promife you that as you and I fifh, and walk to mor-row towards *London,* if I have now forgotten any thing that I can then remember, I will not keep it from you.

Well met, Gentlemen, this is luckie that we meet fo juft together at this very door. Come Hoftis, where are you? is Supper ready? come, firft give us drink, and be as quick as you can, for I believe wee are all very hungry. Wel, brother
Peter,

Peter and *Coridon* to you both; come drink, and tell me what luck of fiſh: we two have caught but ten *Trouts*, of which my Scholer caught three; look here's eight, and a brace we gave away: we have had a moſt pleaſant day for fiſhing, and talking, and now returned home both weary and hungry, and now meat and reſt will be pleaſant.

Pet. And *Coridon* and I have not had an unpleaſant day, and yet I have caught but five *Trouts*; for indeed we went to a good honeſt Alehouſe, and there we plaid at ſhovelboard half the day; all the time that it rained we were there, and as merry as they that fiſh'd, and I am glad we are now with a dry houſe over our heads, for heark how it rains and blows. Come Hoſtis, give us more Ale, and our Supper with what haſte you may, and when we have ſup'd, lets have your Song, *Piſcator*, and the Ketch that your Scholer promiſed fed us, or elfe *Coridon* wil be doged.

Pifc. Nay, I will not be worfe then my word, you fhall not want my Song, and I hope I fhall be perfect in it.

Viat. And I hope the like for my Ketch, which I have ready too, and therefore lets go merrily to Supper, and then have a gentle touch at finging and drinking ; but the laft with moderation.

Cor. Come, now for your Song, for we have fed heartily. Come Hoftis, give us a little more drink, and lay a few more fticks on the fire, and now fing when you will.

Pifc. Well then, here's to you *Coridon* ; and now for my Song.

Oh the braᵥe Fifhers life,
It is the beft of any,
'Tis full of pleafure, void of ftrife,
And 'tis belov'd of many :
  Other joyes
  are but toyes,
   P   *only*

only this
lawful is,
for our skil
breeds no ill,
but content and pleasure.

In a morning up we rise
Ere Aurora's peeping,
Drink a cup to wash our eyes,
Leave the sluggard sleeping;
Then we go
too and fro,
with our knacks
at our backs,
to such streams
as the Thames
if we have the leisure.

When we please to walk abroad
For our recreation,
In the fields is our abode,
Full of delectation:
Where in a Brook
with a hook,
or a Lake
fish we take,

there

there we fit
for a bit,
till we fish intangle.

We have Gentles in a horn,
We have Paste and worms too,
We can watch both night and morn,
Suffer rain and storms too :
None do here
use to swear,
oathes do fray
fish away.
we fit still,
watch our quill,
Fishers must not wrangle,

If the Suns excessive heat
Makes our bodies swelter
To an Osier *hedge we get*
For a friendly shelter ,
where in a dike
Pearch *or* Pike,
Roch *or* Dace
we do chase
Bleak *or* Godgion
without grudging,
we are still contented.

P 2   *Or*

Or we sometimes pass an hour,
Under a green willow,
That defends us from a showr,
Making earth our pillow,
  There we may
  think and pray
  before death
  stops our breath;
  other joyes
  are but toyes
and to be lamented.

Viat. Well fung, Mafter; this dayes fortune and pleafure , and this nights company and Song, do all make me more and more in love with *Angling.* Gentlemen, my Mafter left me alone for an hour this day, and I verily believe he retir'd himfelf from talking with me, that he might be fo perfect in this Song; was it not Mafter?

Pifc. Yes indeed, for it is many yeers fince I learn'd it, and having forgotten a part of it, I was forced to patch it up by the help of my own

in-

invention, who am not excellent at Poetry, as my part of the Song may teftifie : But of that I will fay no more, leaft you fhould think I mean by difcommending it, to beg your commendations of it. And therefore without replications, lets hear your Ketch, Scholer, which I hope will be a good one, for you are both Mufical, and have a good fancie to boot.

Viat. Marry, and that you fhall, and as freely as I would have my honeft Mafter tel me fome more fecrets of fifh and fifhing as we walk and fifh towards *London* to morrow. But Mafter, firft let me tell you, that that very hour which you were abfent from me, I fate down under a Willow tree by the water fide, and confidered what you had told me of the owner of that pleafant Meadow in which you then left me, that he had a plentiful eftate, and not a heart to think fo ; that he had at this time many Law Suites depending, and

that

that they both damp'd his mirth and took up so much of his time and thoughts, that he himselfe had not leisure to take the sweet content that I, who pretended no title, took in his fields; for I could there sit quietly, and looking on the water, see fishes leaping at Flies of several shapes and colours; looking on the Hils, could behold them spotted with Woods and Groves; looking down the Meadows, could see here a Boy gathering *Lillies* and *Lady-smocks*, and there a Girle cropping *Culverkeys* and *Cowslips*, all to make Garlands sutable to this pleasant Month of *May*; these and many other Field-flowers so perfum'd the air, that I thought this Meadow like the field in *Sicily* (of which *Diodorus* speaks) where the perfumes arising from the place, makes all dogs that hunt in it, to fall off, and to lose their hottest sent. I say, as I thus sate joying in mine own happy condition, and pittying that rich mans that

ought

ought this, and many other pleasant Groves and Meadows about me, I did thankfully remember what my Saviour said, that *the meek possess the earth*; for indeed they are free from those high, those restless thoughts and contentions which corrode the sweets of life. For they, and they only, can say as the Poet has happily exprest it.

Hail blest estate of poverty !
Happy enjoyment of such minds,
As rich in low contentedness.
Can, like the reeds in roughest winds,
  By yeelding make that blow but smal
  At which proud Oaks and Cedars fal.

Gentlemen, these were a part of the thoughts that then possest me, and I there made a conversion of a piece of an old Ketch, and added more to it, fitting them to be sung by us Anglers : Come, Master, you can sing well, you must sing a part of it as it is in this paper.

P 4 The

The ANGLERS Song.

For two Voices, Treble and Baffe.   CANTVS.   Mr. Henry Lawes

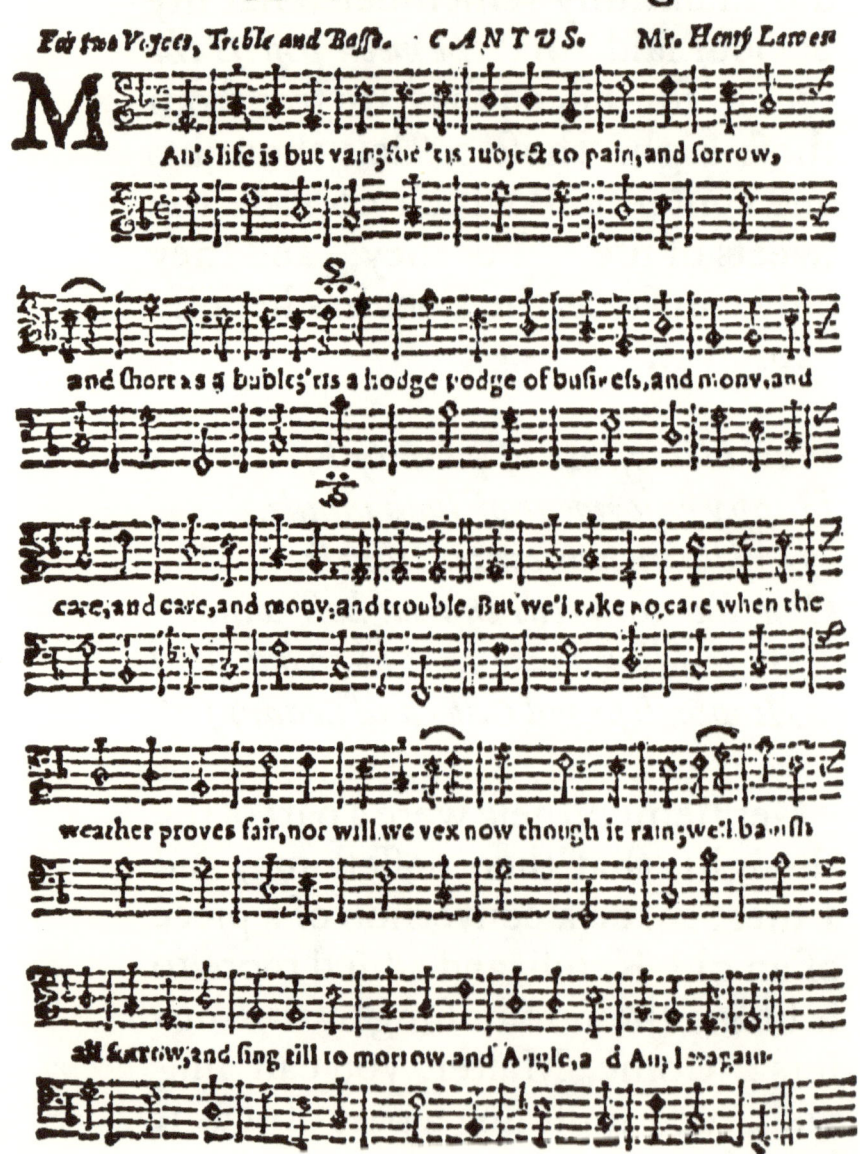

An's life is but vain; for 'tis subject to pain, and sorrow,

and short as a buble; 'tis a hodge podge of business, and mony, and

care, and care, and mony, and trouble. But we'l take no care when the

weather proves fair, nor will we vex now though it rain; we'll banish

all sorrow, and sing till to morrow, and Angle, and Angle again.

The ANGLERS Song.

BASSUS.

For two Voyces.   By Mr. Henry Lawes.

An's life is but vanity, for 'tis subject to pain and sorrow, and

short as a buble, 'tis a hodge podge of business, and mony, and care,

and care, and envy, and troubles. But we'l take no care when the wea

ther proves fair, nor will we vex now though it rains, we'l banish al

sorrow, and sing till to morrow, and Angle, and Angle again.

Pet. I marry Sir, this is Musick indeed, this has cheered my heart, and made me to remember six Verses in praise of Musick, which I will speak to you instantly.

*Musick, miraculous Rhetorick, that speak'st sense
Without a tongue,excelling eloquence ;
With what ease might thy errors be excus'd
Wert thou as truly lov'd as th'art abus'd.
But though dull souls neglect, and some reprove thee,
I cannot hate thee, 'cause the Angels love thee.*

Piscat. Well remembred, brother *Peter,* these Verses came seasonably. Come, we will all joine together, mine Hoste and all, and sing my Scholers Ketch over again, and then each man drink the tother cup and to bed, and thank God we have a dry house over our heads.

Pisc. Well now, good night to every body.

Pet. And so say I.

Viat. And so say I.

Cor.

Cor. Good night to you all, and I thank you.

Pisc. Good morrow brother *Peter*, and the like to you, honest *Coridon*; come, my Hostis sayes there s seven shillings to pay, lets each man drink a pot for his mornings draught, and lay downe his two shillings, that so my Hostis may not have occasion to repent her self of being so diligent, and using us so kindly.

Pet. The motion is liked by every body; And so Hostis, here's your mony, we Anglers are all beholding to you, it wil not be long ere Ile see you again. And now brother *Piscator*, I wish you and my brother your Scholer a fair day, and good fortune. Come *Coridon*, this is our way.

CHAP.

C H A P XII

Viat. GOod Mafter, as we go now towards *London*, be ftill fo courteous as to give me more inftructions, for I have feveral boxes in my memory in which I will keep them all very fafe, there fhall not one of them be loft.

Pifc. Well Scholer, that I will, and I will hide nothing from you that I can remember, and may help you forward towards a perfection in this Art; and becaufe we have fo much time, and I have faid fo little of *Roch* and *Dace*, I will give you fome directions concerning fome feveral kinds of baits with which they be ufually taken; they will bite almoft at any flies, but efpecially at

Ant-

Ant-flies; concerning which, take this direction, for it is very good.

Take the blackish *Ant-fly* out of the Mole-hill, or Ant-hil, in which place you shall find them in the Months of *June*; or if that be too early in the yeer, then doubtlefs you may find them in *July, Auguft,* and moft of *September*; gather them alive with both their wings, and then put them into a glafs, that will hold a quart or a pottle; but firft, put into the glafs, a handful or more of the moift earth out of which you gather them, and as much of the roots of the grafs of the faid Hillock; and then put in the flies gently, that they lofe not their wings, and fo many as are put into the glafs with-out bruifing, will live there a month or more, and be alwaies in a readi-nefs for you to fifh with; but if you would have them keep longer, then get any great earthen pot or barrel of of three or four gallons (which is better) then waſh your barrel with water and honey; and having put into it a quantitie of earth and graſs roots, then put in your flies and co-ver it, and they will live a quarter of a year; theſe in any ſtream and clear water are a deadly bait for *Roch* or *Dace*, or for a *Chub*, and your rule is to fiſh not leſs then a handful from the bottom.

I ſhall next tell you a winter bait for a *Roch*, a *Dace*, or *Chub*, and it is choicely good. About *All-hol-lantide* (and ſo till Froſt comes) when you ſee men ploughing up heath-ground, or ſandy ground, or greenſwards, then follow the plough, and you ſhall find a white worm, as big as two Magots, and it hath a red head, (you may obſerve in what ground moſt are, for there the Crows will be very watchful, and follow the Plough very cloſe) it is all ſoft, and full of whitiſh guts; a

worm

worm that is in Norfolk, and fome other Countries called a *Grub* , and is bred of the fpawn or eggs of a Beetle, which fhe leaves in holes that fhe digs in the ground under Cow or Horfe-dung, and there refts all Winter, and in *March* or *April* comes to be firft a red, and then a black Beetle: gather a thoufand or two of thefe, and put them with a peck or two of their own earth into fome tub or firkin, and cover and keep them fo warm, that the froft or cold air, or winds kill them not, and you may keep them all winter and kill fifh with them at any time, and if you put fome of them into a little earth and honey a day before you ufe them, you will find them an excellent baite for *Breame* or *Carp.*

And after this manner you may alfo keep *Gentles* all winter, which is a good bait then, and much the better for being lively and tuffe, or
you

you may breed and keep Gentle thus: Take a piece of beasts liver and with a crofs ſtick, hang it in fome corner over a pot or barrel half full of dry clay, and as the Gentles grow big, they wil fall into the barrel and fcowre themfelves, and be alwayes ready for ufe whenfoever you incline to fiſh; and thefe Gentles may be thus made til after *Michaelmas* : But if you defire to keep Gentles to fiſh with all the yeer, then get a dead *Cat* or a *Kite*, and let it be fly-blowne, and when the Gentles begin to be alive and to ſtir, then bury it and them in moiſt earth, but as free from froſt as you can, and thefe you may dig up at any time when you intend to ufe them ; thefe wil laſt till *March*, and about that time turn to be flies.

But if you be nice to fowl your fingers (which good Anglers feldome are) then take this bait : Get a handful of well made Mault, and

put

put it into a diſh of water, and then
waſh and rub it betwixt your hands
til you make in cleane, and as free
from husks as you can; then put that
water from it, and put a ſmal quantitie of freſh water to it, and ſet it in
ſomething that is fit for that
purpoſe, over the fire, where it is
not to boil apace, but leiſurely, and
very ſoftly, until it become ſomewhat ſoft, which you may try by
feeling it betwixt your finger and
thumb; and when it is ſoft, then
put your water from it, and then take
a ſharp knife, and turning the ſprout
end of the corn upward, with the
point of your knife take the back
part of the husk off from it, and yet
leaving a kind of husk on the corn,
or elſe it is marr'd; and then cut off
that ſprouted end (I mean a little of
it) that the vvhite may appear, and
ſo pull off the husk on the cloven ſide
(as I directed you) and then cutting
off a very little of the other end, that

Q   ſo

fo your hook may enter, and if your hook be fmall and good, you will find this to be a very choice bait either for Winter or Summer, you fometimes cafting a little of it into the place where your flote fwims.

And to take the *Roch* and *Dace*, a good bait is the young brood of Wafps or Bees, baked or hardned in their husks in an Oven, after the bread is taken out of it, or on a fire-fhovel; and fo alfo is the thick blood of *Sheep*, being half dryed on a trencher that you may cut it into fuch pieces as may beft fit the fize of your hook, and a little falt keeps it from growing black, and makes it not the worfe but better; this is taken to be a choice bait, if rightly ordered.

There be feveral Oiles of a ftrong fmel that I have been told of, and to be excellent to tempt fifh to bite, of which I could fay much, but I remember I once carried a fmall bottle

bottle from Sir *George Haſtings* to Sir *Henry Wotton* (they were both chimical men*)* as a great preſent; but upon enquiry, I found it did not anſwer the expectation of Sir *Henry*, which with the help of other cir-cumſtances, makes me have little belief in ſuch things as many men talk of; not but that I think fiſhes both ſmell and hear (as I have ex-preſt in my former diſcourſe) but there is a myſterious knack, which (though it be much eaſier then the Philoſophers-Stone, yet) is not a-tainable by common capacities, or elſe lies locked up in the braine or breſt of ſome chimical men, that, like the *Roſi-crutions*, yet will not re-veal it. But I ſtepped by chance in-to this diſcourſe of Oiles, and fiſhes ſmelling; and though there might be more ſaid, both of it, and of baits for *Roch* and *Dace*, and other flote fiſh, yet I will forbear it at this time, and tell you in the next place how

yo

you are to prepare your tackling: concerning which I will for sport sake give you an old Rhime out of an old Fish-book, which will be a part of what you are to provide.

My rod,and my line,my flote and my lead,
My hook,& my plummet,my whetstone & knife,
My Basket, my baits, both living and dead,
My net,and my meat,for that is the chief;
Then Imust have thred & hairs great & smal,
With mine Angling purse,and so you have all.

But you must have all these tackling, and twice so many more, with which, if you mean to be a fisher,you must store your selfe: and to that purpose I will go with you either to *Charles Brandons* (neer to the *Swan* in *Golding-lane*); or to Mr. *Fletchers* in the Court which did once belong to Dr. *Nowel* the Dean of *Pauls*, that I told you was a good man, and a good Fisher; it is hard by the west
end

end of Saint *Pauls* Church: they be both honeſt men, and will fit an Angler with what tackling hee wants.

Viat. Then, good Maſter, let it be at *Charles Brandons*, for he is neereſt to my dwelling, and I pray lets meet there the ninth of *May* next about two of the Clock, and I'l want nothing that a Fiſher ſhould be fur-niſhed with.

Piſc. Well, and Ile not fail you, God willing, at the time and place appointed.

Viat. I thank you, good Ma-ſter, and I will not fail you : and good Maſter, tell me what baits more you remember, for it wil not now be long ere we ſhal be at *Toten-ham High-Croſs*, and when we come thither, I wil make you ſome requi-tal of your pains, by repeating as choice a copy of Verſes, as any we have heard ſince we met toge-

Q 3   ther;

ther, and that is a proud word; for wee have heard very good ones.

Pisc. Wel, Scholer, and I shal be right glad to hear them; and I wil tel you whatsoever comes in my mind, that I think may be worth your hearing : you may make another choice bait thus, Take a handful or two of the best and biggest *Wheat* you can get, boil it in a little milk like as Frumitie is boiled, boil it so till it be soft, and then fry it very leisurely with honey, and a little beaten *Saffron* dissolved in milk, and you wil find this a choice bait, and good I think for any fish, especially for *Roch*, *Dace*, *Chub* or *Greyling* ; I know not but that it may be as good for a River *Carp*, and especially if the ground be a little baited with it.

You are also to know, that there be divers kinds of *Cadis*, or *Caseworms*

worms, that are to bee found in this
Nation ir feveral diftinct Counties,
& in feveral little Brooks that relate
to biggerRivers,as namely one*Cadis*
called a *Piper,* whofe husk or cafe is
a piece of reed about an inch long or
longer,and as big about as the compafs of a two pence;thefe worms being kept three or four days in a wool-
len bag with fand at the bottom of
it,and the bag wet once a day,will in
three or four dayes turne to be yellow; and thefe be a choice bait for
the *Chub* or *Chavender,* or indeed
for any great fifh, for it is a large
bait.

There is alfo a leffer *Cadis-worm,*
called a *Cock-fpur,* being in fafhion
like the fpur of a Cock, fharp at one
end, and the cafe or houfe in which
this dwels is made of fmal *husks* and
gravel, and *flime,* moft curiously
made of thefe, even fo as to be won-
dred at, but not made by man (no

Q 4 more

more then the neft of a bird is: this
is a choice bait for any flote fifh, it
is much lefs then the *Piper Cadis*, and
to be fo ordered; and thefe may be
fo preferved ten, fifteen, or twentie
dayes.

There is alfo another *Cadis* called by forne a *Straw-worm*, and by
fome a *Ruffe-coate*, whofe houfe or
cafe is made of little pieces of bents
and Rufhes, and ftraws, and water weeds, and I know not wha,
which are fo knit together with con-
denf'd flime, that they ftick up about
her husk or cafe, not unlike the *briftles*
of a *Hedg-hog*; thefe three *Cadis* are
commonly taken in the beginning of
Summer, and are good indeed to
take any kind of fifh with flote or
otherwife. I might tell you of
many more, which, as thefe doe
early, fo thofe have their time of
turning to be flies later in Summer; but I might lofe my felfe,
and

and tire you by fuch a difcourfe, I fhall therefore but remember you, that to know thefe, and their feveral kinds, and to what flies every particular *Cadis* turns , and then how to ufe them, firft as they bee *Cadis*, and then as they be flies, is an Art , and an Art that every one that profeffes Angling is not capable of.

But let mee tell you , I have been much pleafed to walk quietly by a Brook with a little ftick in my hand, with which I might eafily take thefe, and confider the curiofity of their compofure; and if you fhall ever like to do fo, then note, that your ftick muft be cleft, or have a nick at one end of it, by which meanes you may with eafe take many of them out of the water, before you have any occafion to ufe them. Thefe, my

my honeſt Scholer, are ſome obſervations told to you as they
now come ſuddenly into my memory, of which you may make
ſome uſe : but for the practical part,
it is that that makes an Angler ; it is
diligence, and obſervation, and practice that muſt do it.

CHAP.

CHAP. XIII.

Pisc. WEll, Scholer, I have held you too long about thefe *Cadis*, and my fpirits are almoft fpent, and fo I doubt is your patience; but being we are now within fight of *Totenham*, where I firft met you, and where wee are to part, I will give you a little direction how to colour the hair of which you make your lines, for that is very needful to be known of an *Angler*; and alfo how to paint your rod, efpecially your top, for a right grown top is a choice Commoditie, and fhould be preferved from the water foking into it, which makes it in wet weather to be heavy, and fifh ill favouredly. and alfo to rot quickly.

Take

Take a pint of ſtrong Ale, half a pound of ſoot, and a like quantity of the juice of Walnut-tree leaves, and an equal quantitie of Allome, put theſe together into a pot, or pan, or pipkin, and boil them half an hour, and having ſo done, let it cool, and being cold, put your hair into it, and there let it lye; it wil turn your hair to be a kind of water, or glaſs colour, or greeniſh, and the longer you let it lye, the deeper coloured it will bee; you might be taught to make many other colours, but it is to little purpoſe; for doubtleſſe the water or glaſs coloured haire is the moſt choice and moſt uſeful for an *Angler*.

But if you deſire to colour haire green, then doe it thus: Take a quart of ſmal Ale, halfe a pound of Allome, then put theſe into a pan or pipkin, and your haire into it with them, then put it upon a fire and let it boile ſoftly for half an hour, and then

then take out your hair, and let it
dry, and having fo done, then take
a pottle of water, and put into it two
handful of Mary-golds, and cover
it with a tile or what you think fit,
and fet it again on the fire, where it
is to boil foftly for half an hour, a-
bout which time the fcum will turn
yellow, then put into it half a pound
of Copporis beaten fmal, and with
it the hair that you intend to colour,
then let the hair be boiled foftly till
half the liquor be wafted, & then let
it cool three or four hours with your
hair in it; and you are to obferve,
that the more Copporis you put into
it, the greener it will be, but doubtlefs
the pale green is beft; but if you defire yellow hair (which is only good
when the weeds rot) then put in the
more *Mary-golds*, and abate moft of
the *Copporis*, or leave it out, and take
a little Verdigreece in ftead of it.

This for colouring your hair. And
as for painting your rod, which muft

be

be in Oyl, you muſt firſt make a ſize
with glue and water, boiled together
until the glue be diſſolved, and the
ſize of a lie colour; then ſtrike your
ſize upon the wood with a briſtle
bruſh or penſil, whilſt it is hot: that
being quite dry, take white lead,
and a little red lead, and a little cole
black, ſo much as all together will
make an aſh colour, grind theſe all
together with Linſeed oyle, let it be
thick, and lay it thin upon the wood
with a bruſh or penſil, this do for
the ground of any colour to lie upon wood.

For a Green.

Take Pink and Verdigreece, and
grind them together in Linſeed oyl,
as thick as you can well grind it,
then lay it ſmoothly on with your
bruſh, and drive it thin, once doing
for the moſt part will ſerve, if you
lay it wel, and be ſure your firſt colour be thoroughly dry, before you
lay on a ſecond.

Well

Well, Scholer, you now fee *Toten-ham*, and I am weary, and therefore glad that we are fo near it; but if I were to walk many more days with you, I could ftil be telling you more and more of the myfterious Art of Angling; but I wil hope for another opportunitie, and then I wil acquaint you with many more, both neceffary and true obfervations concerning fifh and fifhing: but now no more, lets turn into yonder Arbour, for it is a cleane and cool place.

Viat. 'Tis a faire motion, and I will requite a part of your courtefies with a bottle of *Sack*, and *Milk*, and *Oranges* and *Sugar*, which all put together, make a drink too good for any body, but us Anglers: and fo Mafter, here is a full glafs to you of that liquor, and when you have pledged me, I wil repeat the Verfes which I promifed you, it is a Copy printed amongft Sir *Henry Wot-tons*

tons Verſes, and doubtleſs made either by him, or by a lover of Angling: Come Maſter, now drink a glaſs to me, and then I will pledge you, and fall to my repetition; it is a diſcription of ſuch Country recreations as I have enjoyed ſince I had the happineſs to fall into your company.

Quivering fears, heart tearing cares,
Anxious ſighes, untimely tears,
  Fly, fly to Courts,
  Fly to fond wordlings ſports,
Where ſtrain'd Sardonick ſmiles are gloſing ſtil
And grief is forc'd to laugh againſt her will.
  Where mirths but Mummery,
  And ſorrows only real be.

Fly from our Country paſtimes, fly,
Sad troops of humane miſery,
  Come ſerene looks,
  Clear as the Chriſtal Brooks,
Or the pure azur'd heaven that ſmiles to ſee
The rich attendance on our poverty;
                              Peace

Peace and a secure mind
Which all men seek, we only find.

Abused Mortals did you know
Where joy, hearts ease, and comforts grow,
   You'd scorn proud Towers,
   And seek them in these Bowers,   (shake,
Where winds sometimes our woods perhaps may
But blustering care could never tempest make,
   No murmurs ere come nigh us,
   Saving of Fountains that glide by us.

Here's no fantastick Mask nor Dance,
But of our kids that frisk and prance ;
   Nor wars are seen
   Unless upon the green
Two harmless Lambs are butting one the other,
Which done, both bleating, run each to his mo-
   And wounds are never found,   (ther :
   Save what the Plough-share gives the ground.

Here are no false entrapping baits
To hasten too too hasty fates
   Unless it be
   the fond credulitie

R

Of

Of silly fish, which, worldling like, still look
Upon the bait, but never on the hook;
*   Nor envy, 'nless among*
*   The birds, for price of their sweet Song.*

Go, let the diving Negro *seek*
For gems hid in some forlorn creek,
*   We all* Pearls *scorn,*
*   Save what the dewy morne*
Congeals upon each little spire of grasse,
Which carelesse Shepherds beat down as they passe,
*   And Gold ne're here appears*
*   Save what the yellow* Ceres *bears.*

Blest silent Groves, oh may you be
For ever mirths blest nursery,
*   May pure contents*
*   for ever pitch their tents   (mountains,*
Upon these downs, these Meads, *these rocks, these*
And peace stil slumber by these purling fountains
*   Which we may every year*
*   find when we come a fishing here.*

Pisc. Trust me, Scholer, I thank
you heartily for these Verses, they be
choice-

choicely good, and doublefs made
by a lover of Angling : Come, now
drink a glafs to me, and I wil requite
you with a very good Copy of Verfes ; it is a farewel to the vanities
of the world, and fome fay written
by *D*ᴿ. *D*, but let them bee writ by
whom they will, he that writ them
had a brave foul, and muft needs be
poffeft with happy thoughts at the
time of their compofure.

Farwel ye guilded follies, pleafing troubles ,
Farwel ye honour'd rags, ye glorious bubbles ;
Fame's but a hollow eccho, gold pure clay,
Honour the darling but of one fhort day.
Beauty (th' eyes idol) but a damask'd skin,
State but a golden prifon, to live in
And torture free-born minds; imbroider'd trains
Meerly but Pageants, for proud fwelling vains,
And blood ally'd to greatnefs, is alone
Inherited, not purchaf'd, nor our own.
  Fame, honor, beauty, ftate, train, blood & birth,
  Are but the fading bloffomes of the earth.

I would

I would be great, but that the Sun doth still,
Level his rayes against the rising hill :
I would be high, but see the proudest Oak
Most subject to the rending Thunder-stroke;
I would be rich, but see men too unkind
Dig in the bowels of the richest mind;
I would be wise, but that I often see
The Fox suspected whilst the Ass goes free ;
I would be fair, but see the fair and proud
Like the bright Sun, oft setting in a cloud ;
I would be poor, but know the humble grass
Still trampled on by each unworthy Asse :
Rich, hated ; wise, suspected ; scorn'd, if poor ;
Great, fear'd; fair, tempted; high, stil envi'd more
　I have wish'd all, but now I wish for neither,
　Great, high, rich, wise, nor fair, poor I'l be rather

Would the world now adopt me for her heir,
Would beauties Queen entitle me the Fair,
Fame speak me fortunes Minion, could I vie
*Angels w*ᵍ *India, w*ᵗʰ *a speaking eye　(dumb*
Command bare heads, bow'd knees, strike Justice
As wel as blind and lame, or give a tongue
To stones, by Epitaphs , be call'd great Master,
In the loose Rhimes of every Poetaster ;
　　　　　　　　　　　　　　　　Could

Could I be more then any man that lives,
Great, fair, rich, wife in all Superlatives;
Yet I more freely would the fe gifts refign,
Then ever fortune would have made them mine
  And hold one minute of this holy leafure,
  Beyond the riches of this empty pleafure.

Welcom pure thoughts, welcome ye filent groves,
Thefe guefts, thefe Courts, my foul moft dearly loves,
Now the wing'd people of the Skie fhall fing
My chereful Anthems to the gladfome Spring;
A Pray'r book now fhall be my looking glaffe,
In which I will adore fweet vertues face.
Here dwell no hateful looks, no Pallace cares,
No broken vows dwell here, nor pale fac'd fears,
Then here I'l fit and figh my hot loves folly,
And learn t'affeEt an holy melancholy.
  And if contentment be a ftranger, then
  I'l nere look for it, but in heaven again.

Viat. Wel Mafter, thefe be Verfes that be worthy to keep a room in
every mans memory. I thank you
for them, and I thank you for your
many inftructions, which I will not
                  forget

forget; your company and difcourfe have been fo pleafant, that I may truly fay, I have only lived, fince I enjoyed you and them, and turned Angler. I am forry to part with you here, here in this place where I firft met you, but it muft be fo : I fhall long for the ninth of *May*, for then we are to meet at *Charls Brandons.* This intermitted time wil feem to me (as it does to men in forrow *)* to pafs flowly, but I wil haften it as faft as *I* can by my wifhes, and in the m ean time *the blefsing of* Saint Peters *Mafter be with mine.*

Pifc. And the like be upon my honeft Scholer. And upon all that hate contentions,and love *quietneffe,* and *vertue,* and *Angling.*

FINIS.